PUFFIN CLASSICS

Underground to Canada

D0071788

BARBARA SMUCKER

Underground to Canada

INTRODUCED BY
LAWRENCE HILL

PUFFIN
an imprint of Penguin Canada Books Inc.

Published by the Penguin Group
Penguin Canada Books Inc., 90 Eglinton Avenue East, Suite 700,
Toronto, Ontario, Canada M4P 2Y3

Penguin Group (USA) Inc., 375 Hudson Street, New York, New York 10014, U.S.A.
Penguin Books Ltd, 80 Strand, London WC2R 0RL, England
Penguin Ireland, 25 St Stephen's Green, Dublin 2, Ireland (a division of Penguin Books Ltd)
Penguin Group (Australia), 707 Collins Street, Melbourne, Victoria 3008, Australia
(a division of Pearson Australia Group Pty Ltd)
Penguin Books India Pvt Ltd, 11 Community Centre, Panchsheel Park,
New Delhi – 110 017, India
Penguin Group (NZ), 67 Apollo Drive, Rosedale, Auckland 0632, New Zealand
(a division of Pearson New Zealand Ltd)
Penguin Books (South Africa) (Pty) Ltd, 24 Sturdee Avenue, Rosebank,
Johannesburg 2196, South Africa

Penguin Books Ltd, Registered Offices: 80 Strand, London WC2R 0RL, England

First published Clarke, Irwin & Company Limited, Toronto/Vancouver, 1977
Published in Puffin paperback by Penguin Canada Books Inc., 1978, 2008
Published in this edition, 2013

2 3 4 5 6 7 8 9 10 (WEB)

Copyright © Clarke, Irwin & Company Limited, Toronto/Vancouver, 1977
Introduction copyright © Lawrence Hill, 2008
Interior illustrations copyright © Vincent McIndoe, 2008

Manufactured in Canada.

LIBRARY AND ARCHIVES CANADA CATALOGUING·IN PUBLICATION

Smucker, Barbara, 1915–2003, author
Underground to Canada / Barbara Smucker ; introduction by Lawrence Hill.

(Puffin classic)
Originally published: Toronto : Clarke, Irwin, 1977.
ISBN 978-0-14-318789-9 (pbk.)

1. Underground Railroad—Juvenile fiction. 2. Fugitive slaves—Canada—Juvenile fiction. I. Title.

PS8537.M82U54 2013   jC813'.54   C2013-902477-8

Visit the Penguin Canada website at **www.penguin.ca**

Special and corporate bulk purchase rates available; please see
www.penguin.ca/corporatesales or call 1-800-810-3104, ext. 2477.

INTRODUCTION BY
LAWRENCE HILL

Some three decades ago, when I was a Grade 8 student in the Toronto area, I became convinced that Canada's past was as boring as boring could be, and that history textbooks had but one purpose—to put one to sleep. My history teacher was deaf in one ear and seemed never to listen with the other, and he spent entire lessons reading out passages about the fur trade while we copied it all in our notepads, word by word. I dropped history after Grade 9, never took another course in it and had to wait some twenty years to discover that history actually fascinated me.

Over the years, as I developed into a writer myself, I learned that there are many ways to bring history to life—to make it exciting and vibrant and immediately important to the reader. There are, of course, many terrific textbooks about history, and they are well worth reading. But drama of the first rank puts a personal stamp on history that allows us, as readers, to feel the pain and sorrows and victories of the characters caught up by huge world events. More than giving us dates and details, historical fiction—when it's well done—helps us understand and feel what it was to live in a certain time and place.

Although I didn't hear about it in my schools as an elementary and junior high school student, the 400-year history of Blacks in Canada is full of drama and action. It reaches back to Mattieu da Costa, a free Black man who came with an expedition that founded Port Royal in present-day Nova Scotia, in 1605. It includes the Blacks—some free, others enslaved—who came to Canada as United Empire Loyalists at the time of the American Revolutionary War. It encompasses the abolitionist movement—led in part by John Graves Simcoe, Upper Canada's first Lieutenant-Governor, who persuaded a reluctant Cabinet (some of whom were slave owners) to institute a partial ban of slavery in 1791 until it was finally abolished in 1834. And it also includes the Underground Railroad, which forms the backdrop of Barbara Smucker's *Underground to Canada*.

Thousands of Black men, women and children escaped slavery in the United States and fled to Canada, aided by "conductors" of the Underground Railroad. There were no real conductors, and there was no true railroad. The railroad and the conductors were simply metaphors for a complex, highly secretive system by which sympathetic people—White and Black—helped fugitive slaves to escape and avoid being recaptured on their long, dangerous run north to Canada. Although fugitives were arriving in Canada via fixed Underground Railroad passages by the 1820s, a major new influx of Blacks escaped north into Canada after 1850, when the American government passed the Fugitive Slave Act, allowing slave owners to recapture fugitive slaves who were hiding in the free, northern States and drag them back south into slavery.

One of the unique and special features of *Underground to Canada* is that its protagonist is a young girl, Julilly, who is ripped away from her mother as a girl and sold to work as a field hand on a cotton plantation in the deep south. Although Julilly is assisted by Alexander Ross (who, in real life, much as we see in the book, was a Canadian doctor who posed as an ornithologist while visiting plantations to advise slaves secretly about how to escape north to Canada), she is a clever and courageous girl who shows great character in her long escape north to St. Catharines, Ontario.

A certain degree of human ugliness exists in *Underground to Canada*. For one thing, readers occasionally encounter the word "Nigger"—two puny syllables whose concentration of fear and hatred is perhaps unmatched in the English language. "Nigger" is a distilled insult if there ever were one. Teachers and parents who read this book with young people have a moral obligation to explain that "Nigger" dates back to days of slavery, and represents an attempt to dehumanize Black people. After all, no slave owner could claim an iota of humanity or respect for God unless he could convince himself that Black people weren't really people, after all, but a sort of sub-species, to be sold and sorted and used and abused like horses and pigs, or worse. The "N" word is offensive to the extreme by modern standards—as was the institution of slavery, and as was the Holocaust. But writers, teachers and parents do no one a favour by pretending that such things didn't exist. Much better to acknowledge them, to understand them, and to ensure that our children and grandchildren are even better equipped than we are to learn from the monstrous mistakes in our past.

At one point in *Underground to Canada*, a man charged with moving slaves from one plantation to another interrupts a conversation between them and some strangers on the road. "Don't you listen to that Quaker Abolitionist and that free nigger boy," he cries out as he whips the men in chains. "They got evil in their words and destruction in their ways." It's an ugly but realistic representation of slavery, and it could serve as a good starting point for discussion at home or in the classroom.

Language aside, it might be said that Barbara Smucker pulls back from describing the full bloodiness of the institution of slavery. Nevertheless, she does provide a few glimpses of just how barbaric slavery was. Julilly is ripped from her mother's arms and sold to another plantation in another state; children are forced to eat cornmeal mush from a dirty trough, pushing and shoving on hands and knees, "sucking and dipping in the yellow grain until there was nothing left." An overseer named Sims savagely whips slaves, including children and old people—every day. However, like thousands upon thousands of other people whose freedom had been stolen, Julilly survives—and, ultimately, embarks on her Underground Railroad trip north to St. Catharines.

Although almost all of *Underground to Canada* unfolds in the United States, Barbara Smucker is to be credited for acknowledging that life in this country was fraught with difficulties for Black people.

Another excellent book for people who are interested in Black history in Canada is *The Narratives of Fugitive Slaves in Canada*. It differs from Underground to Canada, in that it offers lengthy, first-hand accounts by Black people of their own experiences in slavery and of their flight to Canada. Those who want to know more about the experience of slavery, as documented by former slaves, would be well advised to read *The Classic Slave Narratives* (Penguin Books Canada Ltd., 1987), edited by Henry Louis Gates, Jr. It includes four fascinating accounts: *The Interesting Narrative of the Life of*

Olaudah Equiano; The History of Mary Prince: A West Indian Slave; Narrative of the Life of Frederick Douglass; and *Incidents in the Life of a Slave Girl* (the story of Harriet Jacobs).

In the meantime, Barbara Smucker has created a sensitive and dramatic story about a young girl's flight from slavery, and—some three decades after it first appeared in print—*Underground to Canada* still serves as a wonderful introduction to a vital and fascinating element of Canadian history.

NOTE TO THE READER

The escape from Mississippi to Canada by two fictitious characters, Julilly and Liza, could have happened. It is based on first-hand experiences found in the narratives of fugitive slaves: on a careful study of the Underground Railroad routes; and on the activities of two Abolitionists: Alexander M. Ross of Canada and Levi Coffin of Ohio.

I have avoided too much dialect. It is difficult for many readers to understand.

Barbara Smucker

BY MARTIN LUTHER KING JR.

FROM THE MASSEY LECTURES
TORONTO, 1967

It is a deep personal privilege to address a nationwide Canadian audience. Over and above any kinship of U.S. citizens and Canadians as North Americans, there is a singular historical relationship between American Negroes and Canadians.

Canada is not merely a neighbour to Negroes. Deep in our history of struggle for freedom Canada was the North Star. The Negro slave, denied education, de-humanized, imprisoned on cruel plantations, knew that far to the north a land existed where a fugitive slave, if he survived the horrors of the journey, could find freedom. The legendary underground railroad started in the south and ended in Canada. The freedom road links us together. Our spirituals, now so widely admired around the world, were often codes. We sang of "heaven" that awaited us, and the slave masters listened in innocence, not realizing that we were not speaking of the hereafter. Heaven was the word for Canada and the Negro sang of the hope that his escape on the underground railroad would carry him there. One of our spirituals, "Follow the Drinking Gourd," in its disguised lyrics contained directions for escape. The gourd was the big dipper, and the North Star to which its handle pointed gave the celestial map that directed the flight to the Canadian border.

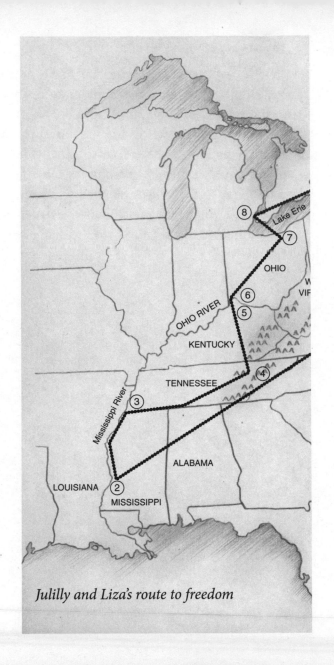

Julilly and Liza's route to freedom

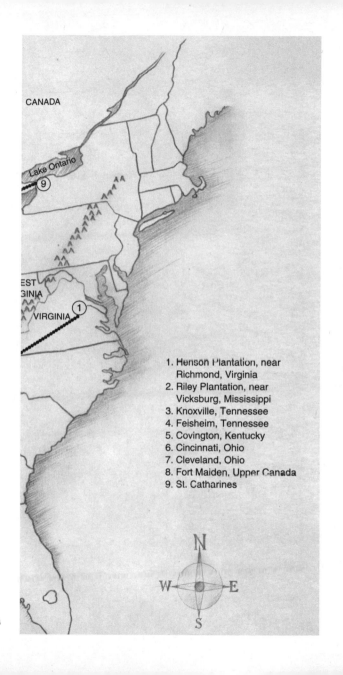

CANADA

Lake Ontario

⑨

EST
GINIA

VIRGINIA ①

1. Henson Plantation, near
   Richmond, Virginia
2. Riley Plantation, near
   Vicksburg, Mississippi
3. Knoxville, Tennessee
4. Feisheim, Tennessee
5. Covington, Kentucky
6. Cincinnati, Ohio
7. Cleveland, Ohio
8. Fort Maiden, Upper Canada
9. St. Catharines

N
W←→E
S

1

Night music droned through the slave quarters of Jeb Hensen's Virginia plantation. The words couldn't be heard but they were there beneath the rise and fall of the melody.

Julilly hummed them as she sat in the doorway of her cabin, waiting for Mammy Sally to come home from cooking in the Big House kitchen. She was as still and as black as the night. The words of the song beat in her head.

When Israel was in Egypt's land
Let my people go
Oppressed so hard, they could not stand
Let my people go.

Old Massa Hensen didn't like this song. He said it came when there were whisperings and trouble around. There were whisperings tonight. They murmured beneath the chirping of the crickets. They crept from ear to ear as soundless as the flickering of the fireflies.

Even though June was just beginning and there was summer heat mixed with honeysuckle sweetness in the air, Julilly shivered. She tried pulling her coarse tow shirt about her knees, but it had long since grown too short. It wasn't that Massa Hensen didn't give her clothes. He was good to his slaves. It was just that she grew faster than any other twelve-year-old on the plantation.

"She's tall enough to work beside the grown women in the cotton fields," Massa Hensen said.

Mammy Sally scolded about this.

"My June Lilly is just a girl that's grown too fast," she pleaded. Grown women had to pick more cotton and they worked longer hours.

It was because Julilly was born in June and Mammy Sally liked lilies that she got her name. Most folk slurred the words together and they came out Julilly. But they didn't for Mammy Sally.

There were no ring games tonight in the dusty yard before the cabin doors. The children whimpered—fretful and uneasy.

Julilly went inside the cabin where she lived alone with Mammy Sally. The flickering pine knot in the corner fire-place held blue flames. They had no warmth. There was loneliness and emptiness inside. When Mammy Sally came, the warmth would spark out in the fire, and the shadows would bring sleep.

The little slave cabin was tight-roofed and plank-floored, as were all the other slave cabins at Massa Hensen's.

"Better than any other slave cabin in all of Virginia," Mammy Sally declared. She liked the Big House, too, where it was cool and wide and the logs were hewn smooth against the walls, and the plank floors were shined and polished.

THE WHISPERINGS that hung in the night-time air had started this morning when Old John, the coachman, drove Missy Hensen into town. Julilly and the other slaves heard about it later.

Missy Hensen sat uneasy and restless in the carriage seat. She talked to Old John of moving North and of selling things. She talked of how her husband, Jeb Hensen, was old and sick and had to go to the hospital in Richmond. She said they had no kin to leave things to.

The land's used up, Old John," she mourned. "It just has no more life to raise tobacco, or cotton, or any other crops."

Old John agreed. He knew that the Masters in Virginia had used the land until it bled and died. They had no crops for sale these days; so they were beginning to raise and sell slaves instead. There was fertile land in the deep,

deep South. The Masters there needed slaves to work their fields.

When Missy Hensen and Old John drove into town, there was excitement on the Court House lawn. Missy Hensen pretended not to see. Old John, who couldn't read, heard the white folks speak of handbills plastered on the Court House door: "WILL PAY TOP PRICES TOMORROW FOR PRIME FIELD HANDS," they read.

Old John's hands trembled on the horses' reins. A slave trader from the deep South was coming to their town to buy tomorrow! Jeb Hensen was making plans to move!

Old John and the other slaves at the Hensen plantation knew about the buying of Virginia slaves. Word of it spread like a wind-whipped flame to one plantation and then another. Rumours spread. Some said the buyer lined the slaves up one by one like cows and pigs. They'd sell a mother to one man and all her children to another.

"In the deep South," folks said, "even the little children tote hoes bigger than themselves, to chop the cotton. Then they get whipped 'cause they don't finish the work the overseer set out for them."

Massa Hensen didn't whip much on his plantation.

"Too soft-hearted," some of the slave owners said.

THIS AFTERNOON when Old John came home from his trip to town, he hobbled straight to the stable boys.

"A slave trader from the deep South is comin' tomorrow." His voice trembled.

The stable boys ran like hopping toads to the children who carried water to the field hands in the cotton rows.

"A slave trader from the deep South is comin'," they whispered.

Up and down the cotton rows the message spread, faster than a winging bird.

Julilly heard, chopping, chopping cotton in the blistering sun. When lunch time came she ran to the Big House to tell Mammy Sally. For one instant Mammy Sally straightened her tall body and lifted her proud head.

"Oh Lord," she said, "we is needin' your protection now."

Then Mammy Sally drew her lips together and was peaceful. Fears, that had flapped around Julilly's head like blackbird wings, flew away. Mammy Sally would take care of her. She was Mammy's only child.

Now the night had come. Julilly huddled shivering near the cabin door. The plank floor of the cabin was warm and dry. The whippoorwill called its evening song and the round, orange moon spread its gentle light. But her feet were cold. Her hands were icy. A strangeness spread about like an uneasy quiet before a storm.

Then Mammy Sally came, her bare feet silent on the soundless dust. She clasped Julilly's hand, but the coldness and the strangeness didn't go away. She pulled Julilly close, bending toward the small blue flame. The light showed indigo across her strong, lined face. It glistened in her troubled eyes.

"June Lilly, child." She spoke softly, rocking slowly back and forth. "You know the slave trader's in our town. Some of the slaves is to be sold."

"Who, Mammy?" Julilly was cold again and shivered.

"There's no way of knowin'." Mammy shook her head. "Massa Hensen's sick and gone away and Missy Hensen says there's no way to keep us all together."

"Most of us have known no other home." Mammy rubbed her hand across the comfort of the floor. "This is where you were born, June Lilly."

Julilly knew all this—how Massa Hensen was better to his slaves than most—how her Daddy died the day that she'd been born from being bitten by a snake—all those things from long ago—safe things that tied together with planting time and harvest time.

Then Mammy stood. She lifted her head high and the white head-rag that covered her greying hair showed soft and a little golden in the firelight. She straightened her shoulders, almost reaching to the top of the cabin door. Her lips drew firm and her eyes pierced deep into Julilly's. In them was the sting that a bull whip makes and the hurt of a wounded possum.

"We've got to pray hard, June Lilly, and if the good Lord can't help us now, we've got to believe He's goin' to help us soon."

"Yes Mammy." Julilly felt pride in this tall, handsome woman.

"There's three things I want to say to you, child." Mammy drew Julilly close again. "Pray to the good Lord. Remember to be proud that you had a strong, fine Daddy and a Mammy that loves you."

Mammy Sally paused. She pressed her mouth against Julilly's ear. "This is secret talk I'm tellin' you now. Hold it quiet in your head and never let it out your mouth. There's a place the slaves been whisperin' around called Canada. The law don't allow no slavery there. They say you travel north and follow the North Star, and when you step onto this land you are free."

Rustling footsteps outside the cabin caused Mammy's arms to stiffen. She pushed Julilly gently away and, lifting her voice, spoke crossly.

"Now, June Lilly, you crawl down on that blanket in the corner and go to sleep. Before you know it, four o'clock will be around and the morning bell will be ringin' for another day's work."

Talking for those who might be listening from the outside was always different from talking inside to those around you. Julilly knew this and smiled. She lay down on the hard floor beside the fireplace and wrapped a thin blanket around her. "Canada." She thought the name again and again inside her head.

The slave trader meant some kind of trouble. But there

had never been trouble on the Hensen plantation. She and Mammy Sally wouldn't be sold.

Julilly yawned and hummed a quiet tune and the unsung words made her smile and forget the trouble-filled day.

Massa sleep in the feather bed,
Nigger sleep on the floor;
When we get to heaven
There'll be no slave no more.

2

Morning came to the slave quarters of Master Hensen's plantation before there was light in the heavy, black sky. It was four o'clock and Master Hensen's old ram horn bellowed and tooted until nobody slept. Frying sowbelly smells from the cabin cooking fires helped wake the children. Julilly reached for a hoecake and a tin cup of buttermilk that Mammy Sally poured. From the barnyard the roosters crowed sharp and clear.

As on every other morning, Julilly smoothed down her crinkly hair and twisted it tight in a knot at the back of her head. But Mammy Sally, who always wore a clean, white head-rag neatly tied, this morning put on a black one in its place. There was no laughter in her full, strong voice as she called to one slave and then another who passed by their door. A worried frown stitched lines across her forehead.

"Child," she said to Julilly in a yearning, mournful way, "there's trouble ahead for us nigger folk today."

Her lips pinched firm and her eyes flamed with angry courage, but her voice stayed quiet. She gathered Julilly's hands into the strength of her long, black, calloused fingers.

"Lord help us," she said. "The field hands are gonna be sold today. You are one of them, June Lilly. You and I could be pulled apart."

Julilly couldn't understand. Mammy Sally couldn't let this happen.

Mammy shook Julilly into listening. "If we are sold apart, June Lilly, and the Lord forbid, don't forget that freedom land I told you about. You and I are strong. We'll get there with the guidance of that star, and the good Lord's help."

A jay-bird voice screeched suddenly outside their door.

"You field-hand niggers. Line yourselves up along this path and don't you loiter." The sound of a zinging whip cut the air. "Some of you ain't gonna chop no cotton today."

Mammy Sally held Julilly close as they walked outside and joined the field-hand line. The man with the jay-bird voice strode back and forth in front of them. He was a big man with a short, thick neck. His cheeks puffed and jiggled as he walked. Julilly noticed that his fingers puffed, too, over the whip that he flicked in his hand. He had a toothpick in his mouth that stuck between two yellow teeth. Julilly didn't like his oily skin. His faded brown hair was tangled and dirty, his baggy pants were streaked with drippings and his little eyes were green and sly.

He strode toward Lily Brown, a shy young mother barely sixteen. She clutched her two-year-old Willie in her arms.

The fat man paused briefly beside her. His tiny eyes narrowed and he rubbed his oily hand down Willie's bare back.

"This is a fat, strong nigger baby," he called to a younger white man behind him. "Put him in the wagon."

Willie was ripped from his mother's arms without a comment.

Lily screamed and fell to the ground.

Julilly started to run toward her, but the firm hand of Mammy Sally grasped her shoulder.

The fat man was stopping in front of them, clamping the toothpick hard between his lips. He stuck a fat finger into her mouth and squinted at her teeth. Satisfied, he pushed back her eyelids.

"Looking at me like Old John does his horse," Julilly thought and flamed with anger.

"This one will do," the big man called toward the young man who had just dumped Willie in the cart. "She's strong and healthy and still growin'. Get over there, girl, and get into that cart." He strode off down the line.

Julilly didn't move. She looked at Mammy, and for the first time in her life saw fear in Mammy Sally's eyes.

"Do like he say, child." Mammy's voice hurt and choked. "You got to mind that man in order to save your life. Don't forget that place I told you about."

The fat man looked back and screeched,

"Get in that wagon, girl, or I'll use this whip and teach you how to jump."

There was moaning now and crying up and down the line of slaves. The big slave trader didn't care or hear. He lashed his whip in the air, pulling children from their mothers and fathers and sending them to the cart.

Julilly moved toward the long, wooden cart. Her feet pulled her there somehow and she climbed inside. She looked for Mammy Sally, but Mammy was already being pushed with the older slaves far down beyond the tool shed.

Julilly strained to find Mammy's black head-rag. It was gone. Mammy Sally had disappeared!

A red sun boiled up into the sky, making patches of heat wherever it struck the uncovered earth. Julilly sat still and numb in the unshaded wagon. Little Willie Brown whimpered beside her. She wanted to comfort him, but she couldn't lift her hand. She found it hard to swallow and wondered if she could make a sound if she tried to speak.

Other children began climbing into the wagon. They were smaller than Julilly. They moved near her— their little bodies twitched like a wild bird she had

caught once and held for a moment before it broke into flight.

Three men were ordered into a line behind the cart. They stood like broken trees, their hands dangling like willow branches in the wind. Julilly knew each one.

There was Ben, solid and strong and as black as midnight. He could chop a woodpile higher than his head when the others still had little mounds up to their knees.

There was kind, gentle Adam whose singing was low as the sightless hollow in a tree. And then there was Lester, the mulatto with speckly skin and angry eyes. Each one had a wife and one or two babies. They didn't move when the fat man with his puffed, oily fingers clamped a chain around their legs.

Julilly watched. The chain became a silver snake. It coiled over the ground, around the men, and up onto the back of their cart. It bit into a lock that held it fast.

Another strange white man led a work-horse in front of them. Julilly was afraid to look at him. She felt the tug and jerk of the wagon and the bounce of the man as he jumped onto the front seat.

"Gid-eee-up," he cried, snapping the reins.

The snake-chain jingled in protest while the men, who were not used to it, tried to swing their bound legs in some sort of order. The fat man, with the toothpick still in his mouth, rode behind them on a smooth brown horse.

They moved down the dusty road, past the empty slave cabins and around by Master Hensen's house. It was empty. There were no curtains in the tall windows or chairs on the wide, shaded porch. Massa and Missy Hensen were gone.

Old John came through the wide front door, hobbled and bent. He shaded his eyes to watch the chain gang and the wagon load of children. When he saw Julilly, his back straightened. Pulling a large, white handkerchief from his pocket, he waved it up and down—up and down—up and down—until it became a tiny speck and disappeared.

Tears ran down Julilly's cheeks. She couldn't stop them, but she made no sound. The fat man didn't notice her.

3

The wagon of slave children jogged slowly down the road. The clang of the chained men behind it took up a rhythm. To Julilly, it was a slow, sad rhythm—sad as the bells tolling a death from the village church near Massa Hensen's.

Julilly could think only of Mammy Sally. Each time the cart turned onto a new road, she expected to see the tall, strong woman with the black head-rag come to take her from the wagon and direct the slaves to turn around and go back to Massa Hensen's. But each new road was empty.

The little children around her wore skimpy clothes. They pressed against Julilly with their hot, dry skin and whimpered like tiny, forgotten sheep. Julilly held two, small hands, both sticky with sweat and dust.

The sun flamed gold and blistering above them, and the sky became hard and bright blue. There wasn't a wisp of cloud to soften it. Julilly saw the white man who drove their wagon wipe his forehead with a large blue cloth. The brim of his hat hid his face, but his neck was red with sunburn. He cracked his whip over the plodding horse. The fat, oily man behind them snapped his whip over the backs of Ben and Adam and Lester who shuffled along with their chains.

The cart jogged past green cotton fields and spreading tobacco plants. Slaves chopped along the rows with their hoes, just as at Master Hensen's. Julilly wondered if they would stop in one of these fields. Why did they go on and on? Where was this "deep South" she heard the slave traders mumbling about?

The sun steamed when it reached the top of the sky and poured down rays of heat over the earth. The children stopped whimpering. Their mouths were too hot and dry for sound.

Julilly watched for patches of shade along the road. But the silent pine and wide-spreading oak trees grew away from the wagon's path. The children asked for water. Julilly wanted water, too. She began to see shimmering pools of water ahead of their cart, but each one disappeared when the wagon drew near it.

The man in the driver's seat sipped from a dirty bottle and water dripped over his chin. The children watched greedily.

The cart began to climb a small hill. At the end of it another, higher hill started. The hills came along like stair-steps. Trees grew thicker and they sucked away some of the heat. A swift moving stream flashed above them, spilling water through the air. The children clung to Julilly and their eyes spoke fear. They had never seen sheets of falling water.

The fat man ordered the driver to stop. His jug needed refilling. There would be a rest.

Julilly was too frightened to move. The chained men dropped onto the ground. With the motion ended, she felt the closeness of the driver and the oily man on horseback. But the fat man ambled away with his horse toward the rushing stream, while the driver climbed from his seat and stretched his body under a tree.

Julilly and the children watched the splashing water. Standing near it was a tall white man chopping wood with a flashing axe. A young black boy worked beside him, stacking the cut logs into a long, neat pile.

With her own need for a drink and her parched, dry mouth, Julilly had forgotten that the children were thirsty too.

"Julilly, get us water."

"Please, Julilly, get us water," they pleaded.

Always before when needs came, Mammy Sally had been there to help. A great ache filled Julilly's throat and the still fear of strangeness crept over her. The fat white man was strange and cruel. The falling water was strange and frightening. Ben, Lester, and Adam were like strangers and they were helpless. Only Lester, the mulatto, raised his head with the same angry eyes. Julilly saw blood on his legs where the chains rubbed back and forth.

The tall man near the waterfall looked up and saw the slave children in the cart. He dropped his axe and began walking toward them, motioning for the boy to follow.

There was no whip in his hand. His face was bony, but gentle. A grey hat circled his head with a large brim, and his long, grey coat had no collar. He walked toward Lester.

"Why are you in chains?" he asked quietly.

Lester pointed toward the sleeping wagon driver under the tree and then to the fat man on his horse far down the stream.

"They took us away from our wives and children. They chained us so we can't escape and go back to them. We've been sold."

The tall man shook his head.

"You need water," he said simply. He turned to the small black boy. "James, fill the large pail with water and bring the drinking gourds."

Within minutes the pail appeared on the road. Gourds were dipped into it, and one by one the men drank. The young boy came toward Julilly and handed her a dripping gourd. He held it for her while she swallowed twice, greedily. Then she stopped, took the gourd from his hands and carefully held it to the lips of each small child.

Julilly wanted to thank him, but she didn't know how.

"Are you the slave of that tall man?" she asked instead.

"No," the boy said quickly, "I'm free. Mr. Fox pays me for stackin' his wood."

Before Julilly could say any more, the fat man came bouncing up the road on the back of his horse. He slapped his whip against the naked backs of the chained men and shouted in anger,

"Don't you listen to that Quaker Abolitionist and that free nigger boy. They got evil in their words and destruction in their ways."

The wagon driver shook himself awake and jumped onto his seat. The wagon began to jog and bump. The chains clanked and scraped.

Julilly looked again at the free black boy. He stood by the tall man and clasped his hands tight in front of him. Tears fell down his cheeks.

A little of the fear and a little of the ache lifted from Julilly. She began repeating the strange words which the fat man had used—"Quaker Abolitionist, free nigger boy . . . Quaker Abolitionist, free nigger boy . . ."—and found herself wondering if the words might have something to do with Canada.

4

One day was swallowed by the next and then the next. The swaying, jogging wagon became a home for Julilly and the little children. Its scraping, clattering noise was a wall closing out the fat man's shouts and the clanging of the torturing chains. Sometimes it was cold when the night came and the wagon stopped on a tall hill with black trees and silver stars and a biting wind that never stopped. The children clung to Julilly and she warmed them as best she could in her thin, strong arms.

When the day came with white-hot sun that baked the road into stifling dust, Julilly cooled the children's mouths with water from the drinking gourd that the free black boy had given her. She always filled it now when the wagon stopped beside a stream and the fat man threw each of them a cold hoecake with a sop of grease on top. She used the gourd, too, for pouring water over the swollen, bleeding ankles of Lester, Adam, and Ben when the white men left them to fish along a river bank.

Julilly seldom spoke. There was nothing to say. But she shared the others' silent fear and anger. Sometimes when the red-necked driver slept, and the fat man strolled off to fish, Julilly thought of jumping from the wagon and running into the woods. But if she did, who would care for the babies in the wagon? Who would pour water over the torn ankles of Lester, Adam, and Ben? She was the only one strong and free enough to help them. She was held, too, by Lester's sullen, glinting hatred and lifted head. His pride brought swish after swish of the fat man's whip across his back. The children cried and the whip poised high above their heads with a threat.

"You shut your little black mouths or this whip comes down on you," the fat man cried.

In response Julilly would sing, slow and soft and deep, and the children listened and remembered their mammies and their cabins at Massa Hensen's. Julilly yearned for Mammy Sally and she sang the songs that she had heard Mammy sing:

I am bound for the promised land.
I am bound for the promised land.
Oh, who will come and go with me?
I am bound for the promised land.

Julilly didn't know why, but somehow she drew strength from Lester's high-held head and angry eyes.

When she woke up cold and frightened during the night on the rough floor of the wagon, she felt better knowing that Lester was close by. He helped her to remember the free black boy and the tall, gentle man who paid him for his work. Most of all, he helped her remember Canada.

One day the wagon slushed through a cypress swamp. The muddy water lay as quiet as a flat, smooth mirror. The trees rose out of it straight and tall and their soft green needles strained the sun like spreading sieves. Flicks and specks of sunlight sparkled on the water. A heavenly sight, Julilly thought, and held her breath with wonder.

But the wet swamp mud sucked down the heavy chains and pulled at the legs of Sam and Adam. They fell splashing and gasping into the water. Lester tugged at their arms, biting his lips against the pain in his own bruised legs. He pulled them out with the bulge of his great muscles. The fat man's whip slapped through the water and onto the wet, muddy backs of the slaves.

A sudden shower of rain splashed through the needled trees. The driver of the wagon hunched his shoulders up to the rim of his wide hat until it made an umbrella over him. The fat man urged his horse ahead of the wagon and huddled under a low branched tree. There was no protection for Julilly and the children or for the struggling men trying to pull themselves from the sucking swamp mud.

With the same suddenness as the onset of the rain, Julilly lost her fear. She had to help the men in the water. Maybe it was like Mammy Sally use to say, "The Lord has made you strong and tall for a good reason." She slid to the end of the wagon and began climbing over the side when she saw Lester standing still and staring at her. His head shook slightly—a warning for her not to come. But his face shifted from anger to a quick smile and his eyes held hers with a look of pride and approval. Lester was proud of her!

Julilly waded into the swamp and pulled up the mud-covered chain. Without its heavy weight the men could lift their legs. The horse tugged at the wagon until it rolled out onto firm, dry ground, and Julilly returned to the little children.

The rain stopped and a gold sun poured a warm circle of light over all of them. Julilly began to sing:

Jenny crack corn and I don't care,
Jenny crack corn and I don't care,
Jenny crack corn and I don't care,
My massa's gone away!

The children smiled and asked her to sing it again.

5

One day the land became flat again and on either side of the wagon, green fields dotted with cotton plants appeared. Up and down the rows, lines of slaves chopped the rich, black soil with their long-handled hoes.

"Looks like we've made it to ol' Mississippi," the fat man called out to the driver who jolted about on the wagon seat.

"Won't be long now." This was one of the few sentences the driver had spoken on the long trip.

Julilly felt both relief and uneasiness. This must be the dreaded "deep South" that Massa Hensen's slaves had all talked about. But it did mean that the wagon would finally stop. Might it even be that Mammy Sally was here?

At a jog in the road, the wagon turned into a lane that seemed to lead straight into a field. The driver and the fat man appeared tense and nervous. They smoothed their hair and tidied their rumpled shirts and stained trousers as best they could.

Then the wagon stopped bumping, as the road became smooth and hard. Instead of brambles and shaggy bushes on either side, there were rows and rows of tall, wrinkle-barked oak trees. Julilly's eyes widened, for hanging from the branches and floating back and forth in the summer breeze, were silent cloud-like drapes of swaying grey moss. It was cool and soft and beautiful and Julilly wanted to catch it in her arms. But the row of trees ended in a stretch of thick green grass. Shading it from every ray of sun were three wide-spreading magnolia trees. Fresh, white blossoms sprang from the heavy waxed leaves. To Julilly they looked like the white linen napkins from Missy Hensen's Big House hanging up to dry. A gentle fragrance filled the air.

Then, Julilly saw the Big House. She stared. It was not at all like Massa Hensen's. Clean, white pillars rose in front of the largest house she had ever seen. They looked as though they sprouted from the earth. And between them, in glistening white, were rows of steps fanned out like a peacock's plume. Two white folks sat on the green lawn in wide frame chairs. The man was tall and thin. Julilly especially noticed that his hair was copper red and that his sharp, trimmed beard matched it exactly. His knees were crossed and his high riding boots shone like pools of muddy water. He flicked a riding whip and laughed at a row of white geese parading over the lawn. The woman was frail and sank back in her chair into the fluffy billows of a pink dress. Neither of them looked in the direction of Julilly's wagon. They barely noticed the fat man who walked toward them until he said, "Mornin' sir." The fat man bowed slightly and waited.

"I see, Sims," drawled the man in the chair, "you've bought us a sorry lookin' parcel of slaves." He glanced briefly at the chained Adam, Ben, and Lester.

"Get them back to the nigger quarters and see that they're ready for work in the mornin."

"Yes sir." Sims bowed again. "Good day to ya'all, Miss Riley—Master Riley."

The fat man backed away toward the slave wagon.

"So," Julilly thought to herself, "this is the Riley plantation and he's the Massa same as Massa Hensen." Then with a shock she realized that the fat man, Sims, was the overseer. He was boss of all the slaves.

The wagon pulled back to a thin road behind the Big House. Weeds and tangled brambles took over between the trees. There was a wide space at the end of the road, but no grass grew on it. The stomping bare feet of hundreds of black folks had packed the earth into a hard, bare floor.

It must be Sunday, Julilly decided, for all the slaves were at home. She wondered if Sunday here would be the same as at Massa Hensen's, a banjo would be scrounged up and washing, cooking, and visiting were done. And maybe, as at Massa Hensen's, a banjo would be scrounged up and dancing and singing would start.

The little children in the cart leaned eagerly over the sides, perhaps expecting to find home and their mammies.

But Julilly drew back into a corner. This wasn't like Massa Hensen's slave quarters. There was no laughter and almost no talk. The old folks leaned idle against the doors of two long rows of tattered huts. The children, with legs scrawny as chicken legs, sat scratching in the dust with sticks and feathers. They had caved-in cheeks that sucked the smiles off their tiny faces. At Massa Hensen's there had been gardens around the huts and a hen scratching here and there. But here the huts were low and ugly. The doors sagged on broken hinges and the walls of logs spread wide where the mud chinking had fallen out.

There was fear and a set, unspoken hatred in the eyes of the slaves when fat, red-faced Sims strode near them. He stopped between the cabin rows and ran the pudginess of his hand over his oily-wet hair.

His jay-bird voice screeched. "Some of you lazy niggers take these boys to the tool house and unloose their chains. See that they're ready for work in the mornin'." He kicked his heavy foot in the direction of Adam, Ben, and Lester.

Julilly's wagon stopped before a low building. It was longer than the other huts.

"Take these babies, Grannie," he sneered at a sullen old woman—dried up like a crinkly brown leaf. She sucked at an empty pipe. A younger woman came forward and carried them one by one into the low house. They whimpered, and reached after Julilly but the woman closed their mouths with her wide, black hand and hurried them through the sagging door.

Julilly began climbing off the wagon to follow them. They were almost like her babies now. Little Willie Brown broke loose from the wrinkled old grannie and grabbed Julilly's skirt. "Julilly," he screamed.

Sims scowled at the two of them with sudden anger.

"Shut that baby's mouth, Grannie," he shouted at the old lady.

She grabbed Willie with one claw-like hand and shut his mouth with the other.

Sims' small eyes appraised Julilly.

"She's big for her age and strong. Put her with the field niggers that ain't got families."

He stretched his whip in the direction of another long cabin. Julilly walked away from the children toward an ugly, long shack and went inside. There was light and air only from the open door and the cracks in the wall. The small space of hard dirt floor seemed packed with girls, each one clinging to a pile of filthy rags. Julilly didn't look for Mammy Sally. She didn't want to find her here.

There was an empty space beside a sullen, hunch-backed girl. Even in the dim light, Julilly could see ugly scars running down her legs and across her cheeks.

"I'm Liza." A soft voice spoke from the deep shadow against the wall.

Julilly sat down beside her.

6

Liza was the only one in the long room of slave girls who offered Julilly any kind of welcome. There was a listlessness about the others that was like sickness.

Liza reached up and touched Julilly's hand. She pulled her down beside her.

"You been snatched from your Mammy?" she asked.

Julilly nodded. Then, for the first time since leaving the Hensen plantation she began to cry. Fat Sims couldn't watch her here. The others in the cabin didn't care.

Liza sat quietly. Julilly's sobs were the only sound in the dark room. The hunch-backed girl drew closer to her and waited. It seemed a long time before Julilly wiped her eyes and was still.

"This is a no-good place," Liza muttered.

Julilly agreed. "You been here a long time?" she asked. It was good talking to someone. In the jogging wagon, she mainly sang to the little children. Fat Sims didn't mind this, but he had scowled when she tried talking with Lester or Adam.

Liza looked at Julilly closely before she answered.

"I came at cotton pickin' time last summer," she said, "sold and bought and throwed in here to live like a pig." Her words were low and soft. Julilly had to strain forward to hear.

Julilly wanted to ask more questions, but she held back: she wasn't sure she wanted to know the answers.

"You been lookin' at my bent-up back and beat-up legs," Liza said bluntly. She seemed to read Julilly's mind.

"Old Sims likes to whip me," she went on. She looked weary and rested her head on her drawn-up knees. "I tried runnin' away. I got caught. Old Sims whipped me until I thought I was gonna die."

Julilly felt a coldness creeping over her. It squeezed her throat and made her breathing come in jumps.

"The slaves at Massa Hensen's place feared it here in Mississippi," she answered her new friend.

Liza suddenly relaxed.

"You know what my Daddy said to me once. He was a preacher where we used to live.

"He said, 'Liza, the soul is all black or white, 'pending on the man's life and not on his skin.' I figures old Sims got a soul like a rotten turnip."

Both girls smiled.

A bell rang, startling the listless girls in the cabin to action. They began wandering out of the door. Julilly and Liza followed.

The bright sun was blinding after the shadows of the cabin. Julilly squinted her eyes and then opened them wide. She wondered if she was really seeing the sight before her. Little children, naked and glistening in the sun, were running toward a wooden trough in the yard. A man poured corn meal mush into the trough from a dirty pail. The children pushed and shoved on hands and knees—sucking and dipping in the yellow grain until there was nothing left.

Julilly stared with disbelief. She began looking for little Willie and the other children who had travelled with her in the wagon. But they weren't there. They hadn't yet learned how to suck their food from a trough like pigs. But Julilly knew that they would soon or they wouldn't eat. She felt sick. Now she understood why the slaves in Virginia dreaded this place called "the deep South." Liza was right. This plantation was a no-good, rotten place to live.

Liza yanked Julilly into the line of older boys and girls. They gathered around a black washpot where collard greens bubbled and steamed, and bits of fat pork pushed to the surface now and then. Each person carried a gourd and dipped it in. Julilly shared Liza's until an old woman came along and handed her one.

There wasn't much talk. There was too much hunger.

Julilly's gourd was empty and there was nothing more to fill her aching stomach but a dipper full of water.

There was no gaiety or bounce in the walk of anyone around Massa Riley's slave yard, Julilly noticed. At Massa Hensen's, on a day off from work, folks collected in little groups to laugh and sing. Here it was like ghosts being pushed around. The slaves were as thin and frail as shadows.

Again Liza yanked Julilly by the arm. This time she pulled her back to the cabin to take off her ragged tow shirt and put on a crocker sack full of holes.

"What's this for?" protested Julilly.

"On Sunday we wash any ol' rags that we wear for the rest of the week." Liza became sullen again. She could have been taken for a bent old woman if one forgot to look at the smooth, black skin of her face and her young, hurt eyes.

The girls dropped their dirty clothes into one of the washtubs in the slave yard and punched them up and down in the steaming water.

"Here's your 'battlin' stick,'" Liza said, handing Julilly a hard solid stick. "Now we just put our shirts on this big ol' block of wood and hit and battle the dirt right out of them."

At last the miserable beaten rags were hung on a rattan vine to dry.

THAT NIGHT Julilly crept into the long, shabby cabin that housed the slave girls who had no parents. She lay down beside Liza who shared her heap of rags. There was no talking; everyone slept. Julilly looked into the dark. She was fearful of the morning, when Sims would be back: Liza said the cotton in some of the fields was ready to be picked. She thought about the little children, about Adam, Ben, and Lester; and she wondered where Mammy Sally was sleeping tonight.

"Lord, help us find each other again," she prayed and went to sleep.

It seemed only a few minutes later to Julilly when a piercing bell clanged through the darkness. Liza pulled her up by her arm and led her out of doors, where a fire was crackling below the black-leafed trees. A line of slaves passed before it. Julilly followed. Each one was given a corn cake and a gourd of water for breakfast. Silently the line continued. This time hands reached out for a pail. Looking inside hers, Julilly saw that it held another corn cake and a cold strip of bacon.

"It's your lunch," Liza whispered; "don't eat it now."

The line went on—women, men, and children all mixed up together. Next they all got crocker sacks—low and baggy—to fasten around their necks. Julilly knew that before that day was done she'd fill more than one bag full of white cotton bolls.

Julilly had been picking cotton for three years now.

The overseer at Massa Hensen's always said how good she was—not breaking the branches off the stalks when she pulled off the blossoms. She could use both hands to snatch at the bolls and put them in the swinging sack around her neck without dropping one upon the ground.

The line of slaves seemed endless to Julilly as they strung along the field behind fat Sims. He swayed back and forth on his horse, flipping a cat-o'-nine-tails whip into the pink sky. Soon the sun would rise and burn up all the pink and coolness of the dawn.

Julilly followed Liza. She saw that the girl limped and that she bent forward, as though her back was trying to push away the burden of her crocker sack.

"Too many whippin's," a slave woman behind Julilly said, pointing toward Liza.

The sun still hadn't risen far when the picking started.

A sharp cry at the far end of the cotton row froze Julilly's hands in mid-air. Fat Sims had dismounted his horse and was flaying his whip over the back of an old, white-haired man.

"He likes to beat at old folks and cripples like me," Liza said in a low voice without lifting her head.

Julilly saw that Liza couldn't reach the high branches with her bent back, so she began pulling the open bolls from the top branches—letting Liza take all those at the bottom. Her new friend gave her a grateful smile.

The sun rose, white and hot, burning at the nakedness

of the ragged slaves. The face of Sims glistened with sweat. It dripped down from the wide brim of his hat. None of the slaves wore hats. There was no shade for their heads.

Sims' anger rose with the sun. When the work slowed, he used his whip. Julilly's fear of the man turned to despair, and then to intense dislike. She had never disliked anyone as much as this fat, squint-eyed Sims. She avoided looking at him. When he came near her she worked steadily and tried to overshadow Liza, who crouched beneath her, pulling cotton from the lower branches.

Once Liza said after Sims had safely passed beyond them, "That man thinks a slave is just like a work-horse. If you acts like a work-horse, you gets along just fine. If you don't—it's the cat-o'-nine-tails on your back."

The work went on—picking, filling the crocker sack—emptying it into baskets—stamping it down. The small lunch and fifteen-minute rest seemed no longer than the time it took for a mosquito to bite.

The slaves still picked when twilight came, and the red sun had slipped away to cool its fire under the earth. The long walk back to the slave quarters was silent, except for the shuffle of tired feet dragging through the dust.

That night it was as dark as a snake hole in the long, low cabin where Julilly and Liza lay on their heap of rags on the hard dirt floor. There wasn't a wisp of wind and the heat of the day stayed inside like a burning log.

Julilly ached with tiredness and hunger gnawed wildly at her stomach. There had been only turnips and a little side meat served for supper. The other slave girls along the floor slept heavily, but Liza was restless. Her hand reached out in the dark and touched Julilly.

"You is a friend," the crippled girl whispered; "no one else ever picked the high cotton that my poor ol' back won't stretch to."

Julilly felt a strong urge to protect this beaten, crippled girl, who had once tried to run away. All alone Liza had run into the swamp—waded into the sticky water and slept with no covering until Sims tracked her down.

Julilly moved closer to her and began whispering to her about life at the Hensen plantation and the sale to fat ol' Sims.

Eventually she repeated her mother's words about Canada and the freedom that country held for every slave. To her surprise Liza had heard about Canada too, and the two girls talked dreamily before drifting into sleep.

7

The hot days of cotton picking went on and on at the Riley plantation. Since the day she had first jogged up the elegant road with the swaying moss hanging from the giant oak trees, Julilly had not seen the fine big house or Massa Riley or his Missus. She knew only the long, low sleeping cabin in the "nigger quarters," and the cotton fields, where the big branches shot out in all directions with blossoming white bolls, popping out like pure white feathers from a thousand swans.

Sims' savage lashings became a part of every day. So far, Julilly hadn't been touched. Her filled basket of cotton at the end of every day always weighed a hundred pounds. She saw that Liza filled hers too. It was a fearful business to tote the baskets of cotton to the ginhouse for weighing and have Sims find them short. The old people suffered most. Twenty-five lashes on the back with the cat-o'-nine tails was their punishment if they didn't meet the measure.

Julilly sickened with each blow.

More and more she and Liza talked of Canada. But they watched that no one listened. There were whippings for any kind of talk of running away. Sometimes, however, the other slave girls in their cabin heard them and offered fearful words of caution.

"When I lived in Tennessee," one girl said, "my Massa said that folks in Canada would skin a black man's head, eat up all his children, and wear their hair as a collar on their coats."

"I hear tell," another whispered, "it's so cold in that country that the wild geese and ducks have to leave there in the winter. It's not a place for men and women."

Another girl said, "Nothin' but black-eyed peas can be raised in Canada."

Julilly tried not to listen. She must keep her mind on just one thought. Mammy Sally said this country was a place where slaves were free and it was a place where they would meet. It lay there waiting beneath the big North Star.

Each night Julilly and Liza searched the shower of stars in the black sky above the slave quarters until they found the brightest one. It stood guard above the row of lesser stars that resembled a drinking gourd.

ONE MORNING there was a sprinkle of rain. Julilly and Liza cooled their feet in a puddle beside the tool house.

"I feel in my bones, Liza," Julilly almost laughed, "that something's happening around here today that's special. Ol' Sims ain't so mean."

The sullen pout on Liza's face shifted to a cautious smile. It gave her a girl's look that had been locked away in old-age misery.

"He maybe had an extra bucketful of breakfast," she chuckled openly.

Julilly warmed to this unexpected humour.

"You don't talk nasty like a snake's hiss," she giggled quietly. "Something sure is different with this day."

The walk to the cotton field was eased by cool, grey clouds that covered the sun, and the furrows between the rows of cotton were soft with mud.

But Sims' good humour didn't last. He was soon shouting threats and warnings against a heavy rain. It didn't come. The clouds eased away as silent as big bolls of cotton, and the sun shot out from under them into a blue patch of sky. The wet earth began to steam and the black mosquitoes, dizzy with moisture, whined about Julilly's face. She couldn't swat at them because her hands had to keep up the rhythm of the picking.

Liza, bent down among the lowest branches, swayed as though she might be sick.

"My back is givin' me misery," she muttered to Julilly without lifting her head.

The sun hadn't reached the top of the sky yet and there

was a row of picking before the short rest and miserly bit of lunch. Julilly wondered if she could bear the bugs and steaming sun a minute longer. This kind of wet heat soaked up all the air.

Suddenly there were sly looks along the cotton rows toward the slave quarters, although the slaves didn't stop picking. A strange white man was walking up the road toward Sims. Beside him was tall, thin Massa Riley. Julilly knew him at once from his copper-red beard. His hair of the same colour was covered with a wide-brimmed hat.

If the strange man was a plantation owner, he didn't look or dress like one. He was dressed more like a Sunday preacher with a long-tailed jacket fully buttoned and a white shirt, starched around the collar. His stomach rounded out in front, but his straight shoulders and brisk walk had Massa Riley panting to keep up with him.

Julilly felt no fear. If he were buying slaves, there could be no worse place to go than Riley's. But he was no ordinary man, she was certain of this.

When Sims slacked his whip and strode toward the man, the slaves slowed their picking ever so slightly. The strange man bowed his head. It was large and covered with thick brown hair, neatly combed straight back from his forehead. He had a reddish beard and a moustache, too.

Massa Riley's slow drawl hung heavy in the hot, listless air and every word he said could be heard along the cotton rows.

"This is Mr. Alexander Ross." He stretched his words out slowly like strands of taffy. "He's come all the way from Canada to study birds in our beautiful land of the South."

Julilly stiffened. Her whole body seemed to shake. The word "Canada" came like a streak of lightning, knocking her off balance. Liza straightened her back and groaned with pain. She wanted to see this man from Canada, too.

Mr. Ross bowed toward Sims. The two of them stood almost an arm's length from Julilly.

Julilly stopped picking. She stared at Mr. Alexander Ross, who appeared to be looking at the slaves instead of seeking birds in the sky. His eyes crinkled with good humour. They were like Old John's eyes at Massa Hensen's plantation. One minute they mourned for a man in misery—the next minute they laughed like the merry tunes of a fiddle. The small, cruel eyes of ol' Sims were always the same.

Julilly had learned long ago from Mammy Sally that it was easy to know the thoughts of a white man by the look in his eyes. A black man learned to keep his thoughts inside his head and pull the shades down over his eyes so the white man couldn't see inside.

"I'm an ornithologist, Mr. Sims." The portly Canadian lowered a shotgun which he carried and extended his right hand to Sims. The handshake was brief. "I want to make a thorough study of birds in this area and I could use several of your slaves to guide me."

Sims wasn't impressed. He scanned the field and began picking at his yellow teeth with a sharp twig.

"Guess you might as well choose them yourself," he scowled. "This is a busy time here, and I can't spare more than two men."

Massa Riley broke in. "Mr. Ross here has enough scientific names for birds to fill a 200-pound sack of cotton." He viewed his guest with a measure of pride. "At dinner last night, he had our guests charmed with his talk."

Julilly continued to stare. The man must be from Canada. His speech as well as his dress was different. His words came out clipped and fast. They jumped along instead of running smooth together like those of all the white men she had ever known.

"I'll let Sims here take care of all your needs." Massa Riley bowed to Ross, waved good-bye and walked away from the fields toward the Big House and the cool green shade of the magnolia trees.

Sims' small eyes focused on Julilly.

"Get to work you nigger girl," he shouted. His whip slashed down across her back. It pained like the sudden sting of a hundred bees. Julilly had seen others whipped, especially here at Massa Riley's, but she had never had the lash come down on her. She bent over and grabbed Liza's arm, preparing for another blow.

It didn't come. Mr. Ross grabbed Sims' upraised arm and led him firmly down the cotton row. He walked straight and fast, all the while pointing to a far corner where a line of young men carried baskets of picked cotton toward the gin.

Julilly doubled the speed of her cotton picking. She was angry and she was afraid. Now that Sims had picked her out as a slave who watched and listened to white men's talk, he would not forget. He would use his whip on her again.

The sun glared with a white heat from the noonday skies. Sims returned to pace up and down the rows with his angry whip. There were cries here and there as he let it fall. Mr. Ross remained in the far corner talking with the young men.

8

The coming of Mr. Ross unsettled the slaves. Julilly felt it like a spark, flitting up and down the rows of cotton. There was something about the way the heavy-chested Canadian had grabbed Sims' upraised hand when he aimed to strike her again that roused a hope in Julilly's mind.

She couldn't talk with Liza. Sims was too close. She began picking quickly, and when she thought it safe, stuffed extra cotton bolls into Liza's low-slung sack. Without moving her head, she could see Mr. Ross talking with one slave and then another. It was a long time before he finally walked from the field with two of them.

The slaves he chose were Lester and Adam. Julilly stopped picking for an instant just to watch. Big, fast-moving Mr. Ross from Canada had chosen Lester and Adam to help him look for birds.

Julilly knew she must talk with Lester soon. Sometimes

on Sundays, she met him in the yard of the slave quarters. He was always angry, but he listened when she talked of home. Once she had told him what Mammy Sally said about Canada. He had listened hard then. His eyes were excited and he had given Julilly that same cautious look of approval that came over his face the day she helped him from the swamp in the rain.

"Don't you talk about this to no one—just to me and to your friend, Liza," he had cautioned.

Tomorrow was Sunday. She would find Lester and ask him about Alexander Ross.

Julilly and Liza finished picking their row. Far ahead of them they could see the big Canadian with Lester and Adam enter the Piney Woods and disappear.

IT WAS DUSK when the picking and weighing of the cotton was finished. Sims was nervous and uneasy as he checked the scales. Mr. Ross was back and Lester and Adam had been sent to carry baskets of picked cotton. Mr. Ross held his shotgun loose. The grey wings of a dead mockingbird stuck out from a bag that he hung over his big shoulders. Even though he had been tramping about most of the hot afternoon hunting birds, his thick brown hair and preacher-looking suit were as neat and orderly as though he'd been sitting under the shade trees of the Big House lawn.

He stood near Sims.

"Now tell me, Mr. Sims," he asked with his fast clipped Canadian accent, "how much does each slave pick during the day?"

Sims mumbled an answer.

"An amazing crop." The Canadian patted his great stomach and chest. "You know it's too cold in Canada to raise cotton."

Sims perked up with this comment.

"I heard tell," Sims grinned, his upper lip flattened against his yellow, uneven teeth. "it's such a cold place that nothin' but black-eyed peas can be raised there."

Julilly saw a smile flicker on the big man's face.

JULILLY AND LIZA, with the other slaves, trudged back along the dusty path to the slave quarters with lighter steps that evening. As though in some kind of celebration, a large black kettle swung over a crackling flame in the yard. It bubbled with greens and sparse strips of salt pork. There hadn't been greens to eat since Julilly came to the Riley plantation on the first day. She reached inside her crocker bag for the gourd that she always carried with her, ladled out a portion for herself and poured some for Liza into a tin plate.

"Without you, Julilly"—Liza raised her tired head where she sat resting against the trunk of a thick oak tree—"I'd starve to death."

THAT NIGHT in the long slave cabin, all the girls whispered about Canada and Mr. Ross. Most of them knew about the place. Word of it had crept along the plantation "grapevines" in the places where they came from—in Virginia and North Carolina. They shared what they had heard.

Liza knew the most. Usually she was quiet and sullen after the day's work, but tonight she felt like talking. She hunched her crippled back against the pile of rags to ease the constant pain.

"This country is far away under the North Star," she whispered hoarsely. "It's run by a lady named Queen Victoria. She made a law there declarin' all men free and equal. The people respects that law. My daddy told me that, and he was a preacher."

A girl down the line named Bessie, who was tall and strong like Julilly, moved near Liza.

"How you know where to find that North Star, girl?" she asked.

Liza answered with certainty and precision. "You look in the sky at night when the clouds roll back. Right up there, plain as the toes on my feet, are some stars that makes a drinking gourd." Night after night Julilly and Liza had been watching it when the stars hung low, sparkling and glistening.

"The front end of that drinking gourd," Liza went on, "points straight up to the North Star. You follow that. Then you get to Canada and you are free."

"Don't you talk so much, girl," Bessie's whisper was sharp now and strained with fear. "Look what happened to you when you tried to get your freedom. You got a bent back and your legs got all beat up. I ain't lookin' for no more whippin's than I already get." She rolled onto her rags and was soon asleep.

Another girl near by crept close to Liza and Julilly. She was a timid girl, hunched up like a little mouse caught in a corner.

"I'm afraid," she shivered. "I heard a man say once that Canada is a cold country. Only the wild geese can live there. I'm afraid to go. I'm always afraid." She began to whimper. Julilly reached for her hand and held it until the girl went to sleep.

By now the other girls, sprawled along the floor, were too drained and dulled by the daily work and scant food to care or listen. Their exhausted bodies needed sleep. Like work-horses, they found their stalls each night and fell exhausted into the heap of tangled, ragged blankcts.

But Liza hadn't moved from her hunched position against the wall. She wasn't asleep. Julilly could see her open eyes in the soft moonlight that spread through the cracks and open doorway of the cabin. It was late. The only night sounds were the chirping of the crickets.

Every muscle in Julilly's body ached. She spread out flat on her back close to Liza, unable to close her eyes. The thoughts in her head jumped around like grasshoppers.

Was Liza trying to reach Canada and freedom when Sims tracked her down?

Free, thought Julilly. Free must be like a whippoorwill that could fly here and there and settle where it pleased . . . free could mean to get paid for your work like white folks . . . free was like the free black boy who stood beside the tall Abolitionist on the road to Mississippi and gave her water . . . if you were free, you wouldn't be whipped.

Julilly couldn't stop her thoughts.

She finally murmured to the silent, staring Liza.

"Liza." Julilly barely moved her lips. "You thinkin' of tryin' to run away to Canada again?"

She felt Liza's body twitch. Slowly the crippled girl slid to the floor and put her mouth against Julilly's ear.

"You is my friend, Julilly." She barely made a sound. "What I is goin' to say must not be told to anyone."

Julilly nodded her head.

"Before the cotton is finished bein' picked, I am gonna slip away from here some night."

"Are you afraid?" Julilly had to know.

"I am afraid, and I am not afraid." Liza's bony fingers clasped Julilly's arm. "Like my daddy said to me, 'Liza, in the eyes of the Lord, you is somebody mighty important. Don't you ever forget that.'"

Julilly nodded again.

"I'm scrawny, Julilly, but I'm tough. I think the Lord

put that North Star up in the sky just for us poor niggers to follow, and I intends to follow it."

There was a long silence between them.

Finally Julilly said slowly, her heart beating so fast she thought it might snap off from whatever held it in her chest, "I am goin' with you, Liza. I'm afraid and I'm not afraid, same as you."

9

Julilly had always looked forward to Sunday on the Hensen plantation. It was rest time from work. Sometimes a preacher came to an empty cabin that the black folks called their church. There was preaching and singing.

On Saturday nights there was dancing. The slaves went far back into the woods for this, to another empty cabin. Massa Hensen didn't mind, so long as he didn't have to listen. There was plenty of ruckus with Lester and Adam playing the fiddles and Ben banging a set of bones. In her hair Julilly wore a red ribbon which Mammy Sally scrounged up for her. She could dance longer than anybody there.

But things were different at Massa Riley's place. He wouldn't allow a preacher, and Sims whipped anybody he found dancing. Mostly everybody was too tired and too sickly to care. Sunday was washing day and cooking day at Massa Riley's.

ON THIS SUNDAY, Julilly and Liza sat on the ground near the boiling clothes kettle, beating their clothes with battling sticks. They hadn't been able to talk at all about last night's pledge. There were too many people around and there was too much to do.

Julilly felt a new bond between them—stronger than just being good friends. It was held tight by the promise to run away together. It was the most solemn promise Julilly had ever made.

A lazy bee buzzed around her head. She reached up to swat it, and saw Lester. He looked at her steadily and made a motion that she should join him. He shuffled past her without a word and walked down the dusty path, turning behind a row of cypress trees.

"Liza," Julilly whispered, "somethin's happened. Lester wants to see me. Hold my stick. I'll be right back."

"Lester looks upset." Liza had seen him too.

Julilly walked quickly toward the cypress trees. Lester was standing behind one of them—impatient and edgy. Julilly joined him.

"I'll talk fast, Julilly," he said in his steady, bitter way. "Massa Ross from Canada isn't here to catch birds. He's here to help slaves escape to Canada."

Julilly grabbed Lester's arm, but Lester moved away from her.

"I don't want no one seein' me talk to you. Massa Ross is meetin' tonight with some of us in the middle of the

Piney Woods. It's gonna be late—when most folks are asleep. Listen for three calls of the whippoorwill, then walk to this tree. You come and bring Liza. I'll take you to the meetin.'"

Lester left her, walking fast toward the slave quarters where the young men gathered. Julilly returned to the washing, taut and breathless. She whispered the message to Liza at once. The hunched, bony girl scarcely moved. She dropped the battling stick, which scraped over the dust, a hard, twisted branch of oak, unyielding against the constant whacks upon the dirty clothes.

"That stick seems as tough and skinny as you, Liza." Julilly grabbed it up and began pounding at the clothes. It was no good having the others look at them right now. Liza was in some sort of trance.

When she looked up, though, the crippled girl's eyes snapped and danced. They lit up her face until there wasn't a scowl left.

Julilly stared. Liza must be about thirteen years old— the same as her! She hadn't thought of any age for this new friend of hers. She'd just seen a worn-out, sullen, old slave face on her, such as many of the other young girls had.

"You look happy," Julilly said eventually, beating hard with her stick to make up for Liza's not moving at all.

"I am." Liza still didn't move. "I thought my daddy was wrong. I thought the Lord had passed me by. But he hasn't. This time I'll have help in findin' my freedom. I'll have you and Massa Ross."

IN THE SHADOW-FILLED MOONLIGHT that night, Liza and Julilly lay quiet on their cabin floor. Their eyes were closed and they didn't move. Honeysuckle sweetness from the Big House lawn drifted through the open door; gentle bird calls sounded from the cypress grove. They waited and waited, wondering when the call they were listening for would come.

The big girl, Bessie, near by, twisted about and then sat up to swat a mosquito that circled her head.

"Oh, Lord, put Bessie to sleep," Julilly prayed.

Within minutes the big girl did sleep.

Then they heard it—three soft calls of the whippoorwill.

Swiftly and silently the girls crept out of the door. They were barefoot and the hard dirt of the slave quarters made no sound. Lester's shadow spread over the ground near the line of trees, guiding them.

As they approached, they could see Lester put his fingers over his lips. They didn't speak. Lester started walking fast toward the Piney Woods and motioned for the girls to follow.

Inside the woods, the thick, fallen pine needles were soft to their feet. There was no path. Lester meandered dog-like around the tall trunks as though sniffing his way.

They walked deep among the trees until the tall, guarding trunks enclosed them in an open space. Mr. Ross was there with Adam and Ben.

"This is Julilly who I told you about," Lester said breathlessly to Mr. Ross. "And this girl is Liza. She tried to escape once, but got caught. Massa Sims lashed her almost to death."

Mr. Ross shook Liza's hand and then Julilly's. Julilly hadn't expected this. It was a gesture of friendship. It was like their hands made a bridge. Maybe, with this big man's help she could cross over it into Canada.

Mr. Ross drew the group close together. He spoke directly and forcefully. Julilly had to strain to understand his Canadian speech.

"Lester has chosen you out of all the miserable slaves on this plantation," he said, "because he thought you were the only ones with the desire and the courage to escape to Canada."

"That's right for me," Julilly answered gravely. The others nodded their heads.

"My conviction is that human slavery is such a monstrous wrong that any measure is justified to liberate as many of you as possible."

Lester interrupted. "I think these folks should know, Massa Ross, that you are one of those Abolitionists who are helpin' to free the slaves."

"That's right, Lester." Mr. Ross' eyes became merry

and he laughed softly. "I've been called 'Negro Thief,' and in one town in Tennessee a sign was put up which said, '$1,200 reward for the apprehension of the Accursed Abolitionist.' That was me."

His laugh eased the tension. The circle of sturdy pine trees closed about them like a sheltering arm.

Mr. Ross began speaking straightforwardly. "This is a great risk you are taking to escape bondage for freedom. None of it is going to be easy. It won't even be easy when you get to Canada."

He looked at each of them steadily and in turn they met his eyes with lifted heads.

"It takes courage and determination and a good deal of wit." His words were measured and slow. "If you don't think you can do it, I will understand."

Julilly found it strange just to look in the eyes of a white man. How was she going to speak her mind in front of one? She was glad for the night and the darkness that covered all of them.

"I'm afraid, Massa Ross. But I don't want to be whipped by Massa Sims one more time. Even a horse shouldn't be whipped the way he whips us slaves. My Mammy told me to join her in Canada and I want to do this. I've got courage the same as she has."

"That's so, Massa Ross," Lester added. "She helped me out of a swamp when the chain was round my ankle."

Julilly was pleased that Lester remembered. She knew

Lester would never stay at Massa Riley's place even if he was whipped until he nearly died. She didn't know about Adam. He was meek and gentle. He mostly liked to sing. But he had strong arms and a proud head. His skin was as black as Liza's. It faded into the night.

Liza straightened her back and stood as tall as she could. "The Lord has been speakin' to me, Massa Ross," she said simply. "He says to me 'You ain't meant to be beaten. You is a woman same as Missy Riley.' Bein' black don't make me no animal. I got eyes, and hands, and legs same as she has."

Adam was the last to speak.

"Until I met you, Massa Ross," he murmured in his soft, easy way, "I figured white folks had slaves everywhere."

"Those are noble speeches, Liza and Julilly. You are the kind of people we need." Mr. Ross stroked back his thick, reddish hair. "The men have already talked with me. Adam and Lester are certain that they want to go. Ben hasn't decided."

He drew the group closer together and began giving them directions: they must not talk with anyone else on the plantation about the planned escape—they must meet at this same spot next Saturday night and be ready to leave—Lester would give the whippoorwill call again—Lester would be with Mr. Ross all week getting instructions while they hunted for birds—Liza and Julilly would let Lester cut their hair and dress as boys in the woods after they left—their dresses would be thrown in the swamp water.

The eerie call of a hoot owl echoed through the tense, shadowy night. The slaves and Mr. Ross took it as a warning that they should return to their sleeping quarters. They parted in three directions, the girls following Lester on his zig-zag path through the Piney Woods.

10

On their row of cotton the next day, Julilly and Liza kept their heads low and didn't talk. They worked hard, filling and refilling the big basket at the end of their row with soft, white cotton bolls from the gunny sacks slung about their necks. They didn't want to anger Sims. When they saw Lester or Adam, they pretended not to notice them.

There was no more Canada-talk in the long cabin where they lived. At night when the others slept, they tried to sleep too.

"We need to build up our strength," Liza told Julilly. "We need all the sleep we can get."

Julilly couldn't seem to keep her feelings tucked inside as Liza did. Her heart jumped like a scared rabbit. Everything around seemed sharp. The firefly's flickering turned to hot, bright sparks. Grasshoppers scraped the air when they leaped. Their little eyes bulged. Droning cicadas cackled, and cackled, and cackled.

"Keep prayin'," Liza told her.

She did.

The two girls began storing things away on a high dark shelf of the cabin—extra hoecakes, their winter shoes. Massa Ross promised to find the boys' clothes. Lester would have the scissors to clip their hair. On the night before leaving they would stuff their crocker sacks with the few belongings that they owned and hang them over their backs as knapsacks.

The heavy dank heat of August pressed down on the Riley plantation. Thick air hung over everything, filled with magnolia fragrance and the crazed whine of mosquitoes. Sweat trickled over the face of the angry Sims. He whipped at the old and the young without reason. Misery was everywhere—everywhere but on the cool greenness and the pillared whiteness of the Big House. The Big House, poised, serene and stately, ignored the slave quarters.

On Saturday, there were puffs of clouds in the sky. The flies stung and swarmed, as before a rain. Julilly and Liza watched with fear. If a storm blew up, would they go? If the clouds piled high, could they see the North Star?

All day long they picked in the cotton fields. There was no sun and the air was windless. Before weighing started in the late afternoon, Lester appeared with Mr. Ross. The kindly gentleman was as calm and neatly dressed as on the first day of his arrival. This time his bag for birds bulged with specimens.

"Ah, there you are again, Mr. Sims," he called out with a jovial smile. "I've had an excellent day. There are unbelievably rare and beautiful birds in this great land."

Sims looked with disdain at the bag of specimens. Julilly watched Lester. With a quick look, he moved his head slightly up and down three times. They would go! Even if it rained and the clouds blotted out every star, they would go!

Julilly lifted her head and stood tall and straight. This was the last time she would stand shaking and grovelling before Massa Sims, waiting for him to weigh her basket of stamped-down cotton. This was the last time Liza would be whipped and kicked like some worn-out dog.

The two girls walked one behind the other down the path from the cotton fields to the slave quarters. They were silent, but their thoughts were a cord binding them closer and closer together.

When night came, a twisting wind blew the clouds away. It swirled and tussled through the tall pines and then died in some distant field. The slaves grumbled. Rain would have given them a day of rest from the heat and the fields. For Julilly, Liza, Lester, and Adam it was a blessing straight from the Lord. The Big Dipper appeared above them, as faithful as the rising sun, and the North Star sparkled.

"The North Star's been polished by the wind and the rain," declared Julilly to Liza as they hurried to the sleeping cabin before the other girls arrived. They stuffed their meagre supplies into the sturdy crocker sacks, rolled them tight and covered them with the blanket-rags on the floor. Then they lay down and put their heads on top of the pile.

"Close your eyes like you're already asleep," Liza murmured to Julilly as the other slave girls began to drift through the open door. There was little talk, for the day had been long and hard. Julilly felt for Liza's bony, rough hand. Slowly bodies fell silent all over the room, and the night sounds took over.

Julilly found it hard to keep still. Her legs wanted to twist about. Her arms felt like flinging themselves upwards. She clamped her teeth together to keep from shouting: "Let's go, Liza. Let's go!"

She squeezed her friend's hand. The return pressure calmed her. No matter what happened, no matter if Massa Riley got bloodhounds to chase them, she would help Liza, and Liza would help her. And, above all, Liza seemed certain that the Lord was on her side this time. Julilly almost relaxed into sleep when the whippoor-will song sounded faintly three times. The girls lifted their heads slowly, quietly reached for their blankets, and soundlessly walked from the cabin door. Lester was standing by the cypress trees as before. They followed him along the roundabout path in the woods, but this time he went faster and there were more twists and turns.

Julilly knew why. If bloodhounds began sniffing their trail, it would take them longer to wind around the trees.

Massa Ross stood as last time, splendidly dressed and neatly combed and brushed. He didn't seem fearful, even though Liza had told Julilly that he could be hanged for helping them escape. His filled-out chest and big stomach seemed to give him strength.

Adam was there, sitting on the ground, waiting and tense—fox-like—ready to spring. But there was no sign of Ben.

Massa Ross asked them to stand close around him. His voice was lower and softer than before. He clasped each of their hands and said,

"The difficulties and dangers of this route and the inevitable pursuit for weeks by human foes and possibly bloodhounds require the exercise of rare qualities of mind and body. Each one of you has these. You have foresight and great courage."

Julilly liked the sweep of his fine words, even though she couldn't understand all of them.

Quickly, however, he changed his style. He looked about the circle of trees and listened for many minutes to the strange night sounds. When he spoke next, only the four of them could possibly hear.

"You will start at midnight," he said. "Then everyone will be asleep. I have given Lester a watch so that he will know when the time comes. Make it to the swamp just ahead and wade through the low water in your bare feet. This will kill the scent of tracks. Bloodhounds lose their scent in water."

He paused again for a brief moment to listen.

"Tonight you will follow the great Mississippi River north. It will guide your feet and the North Star above will guide your eyes."

He began talking more quickly. The moon was nearing the height of its climb across the sky.

"By all means, stay together. Lester will be your guide. Trust him. I have given him many directions. You will travel by night and sleep by day. When you cross the border into Tennessee, I will be there. Pretend you don't know me and don't be astonished at my face, for my beard will be shaved."

He stopped talking and handed each of them two dollar bills, a knife and some cold meat and bread. To Julilly and Liza he gave a pair of pants and a shirt.

"Change these after you cross the swamp," he said. "Let your old clothes float on the water. The slave hunters might think you have drowned. Lester has scissors to clip your hair short."

He shook hands with each of them, clasping them tightly.

"Now I must go back to the Big House. Tomorrow I leave for another mission in Columbus, Mississippi. Bless you."

He walked swiftly away from them through the shadow-filled forest.

"Massa Ross is a good man." Julilly spoke for all of them.

When they could no longer hear his footsteps, Julilly, Liza and Adam turned to Lester.

"Put everything he gave you in your crocker sack and fasten it to your back," he said. There was no expression on Lester's face, but Julilly saw fear and excitement in his eyes.

He looked at the watch, round and smooth in his hand. It was time to go.

"No one is huntin' for us tonight," Lester said. "We got to cover a lot of ground."

Julilly glanced at Liza. Her head was down, and her back was bent, which meant that it was already hurting her.

"I'm gonna walk by Liza," Julilly stated firmly. "We've agreed to help each other."

"You take the rear, then, Adam." Lester seemed to agree and they started off.

The ground was dry and soft for a stretch and then the wetness came. The lank swamp grass whipped their legs and their feet sank deep into the oozing mud beneath. Julilly grabbed a drooping willow branch with one hand to keep her steady; with the other hand she held Liza's arm, guiding the bent girl along beside her.

Julilly was grateful for the soft moonlight. It illumined dead branches jutting from the water and water-knees protruding from the tall swamp cypress.

Twice she felt the shell of a turtle slip under her feet.

"I hope those old alligators and water-moccasins are sleepin' tonight like they are dead," Julilly whispered to Liza.

"Don't put your mind on things such as that," Liza whispered back. "And don't forget, no bloodhound can smell our scent through this ol' swamp water."

At last the ground became more solid. Then it was dry again. Now was the time for Julilly and Liza to change into their boys' clothes and throw the worn tow shirts on top of the swamp water. Lester quickly clipped their hair with scissors from his knapsack.

There was no time at all to giggle over their changed appearance. Lester was impatient to go on. Already they could hear the flow of the great Mississippi River. None of them had seen it before—but Massa Ross had told them how it would sound and how it would be muddy and fast-flowing and how they would walk north along its banks away from the running current.

When they came to the shores of the river, they stopped. It was an awesome sight. As far as they could see, mud black water rolled past them—broken now and then with eddies and splashes that caught silver from the moonlight.

Adam bent down and eased his hand into the water.

"It's warm and gentle-like," he smiled. "It holds no harm for us, and I smell catfish in the wind that blows right out of it."

"That's good to know, Adam." Lester paced nervously along the shore, looking upstream. "We'll remember about those fish later. Tonight we have bread and cold meat for our meal." He started walking ahead through the dry canebrakes and tangled shrubs, expecting the others to follow.

Julilly watched Liza hunched against the trunk of a sheltering willow. Her face showed pain.

"We're goin' to rest a bit, Lester," Julilly stated. "And Liza and I are goin' to have a piece of our bread and a drink of that catfish-smellin' water."

Lester waited ahead of them on a dry log. Adam cooled his feet in the rushing river. Liza closed her eyes gratefully, accepting the piece of bread and gourd of water that Julilly offered her.

It was a short rest.

"We're ready now." Julilly stood and reached for Liza's hand, pulling her slowly to her feet.

"I'm leading us back a ways from the river," Lester called. "The trees are thicker and the brush is thinner."

They walked on as before, Lester in the lead, Julilly and Liza between them, and Adam behind, humming softly and making a rhythm for their steps. There was no stopping now. The running waters of the Mississippi filled their ears, and the North Star gleamed above them.

Not until the night began melting into the black earth and a streak of pink rimmed the eastern sky did Lester stop. The giant trunks of two fallen pines blocked their path. Underneath the solid logs was a rippling brook of clean water, and beside it a hollow place almost hidden by the rotting limbs.

"This is where we eat and where we sleep," Lester yawned, finally exhausted. The others agreed. They ate slowly, putting aside a portion for the next day's meal. Julilly passed her gourd from one to the other. The water they dipped up with it was cold and sweet and there was plenty.

"Adam and I will take turns staying awake on guard until sunhigh." Lester's eyes followed the widening pink strip along the sky. "Then, Julilly, you and Liza will watch until sundown."

"Thank the Lord that we've had one safe night." Liza bowed her head briefly. "I ask you, God, keep special watch on us tomorrow when Massa Sims finds out we are gone, and starts out lookin' for us."

The others were silent.

Julilly and Liza crawled into the hollow place beneath the logs and slept. They were too exhausted to say a word.

At sunhigh, when Lester shook Julilly's shoulder, she sat up frightened and confused. Had she overslept? Was

Massa Sims ringing the morning bell on the plantation? Why were her feet so sore and bruised?

Then she saw Lester's drawn, tired face and she knew where she was. It was her turn to watch and soon it would be Liza's. Adam lay face down on the soft grass beneath a sheltering willow near the fallen logs.

"If you hear any noise at all, you wake me, Julilly." Lester rubbed his long fingers over his eyes to smooth out the tired lines.

"You can trust me, Lester," she answered.

"And when the sun goes down, we'll eat. Adam caught some catfish—just like he said. He cleaned and skinned them." Lester smiled.

"Someone will see if we start a fire to cook them." Julilly was alarmed.

"Massa Ross told me how to do it," Lester answered calmly. "He said, build a fire in a clear place far away. Then watch. If nobody comes, just lay whatever you catch on the hot coals. When they die down, the fish is ready to eat."

Julilly smiled too. She settled herself on a scattering of dry pine needles, behind a tangle of brambles and dead limbs and waited. Liza looked bent and shrivelled lying asleep near by. Twice she moaned, but didn't wake.

"I'm strong enough to watch for both of us," Julilly decided. "She better rest her aching back."

A mockingbird sailed through the sky, then perched

above her and sang its own clear song. A gentle deer walked serenely to the river's edge and dipped its head for a long drink.

It was peaceful to sit so quiet. But it didn't last. The deer jerked its head upright. It listened and then ran back among the trees. The mockingbird chirped a mixed-up song of many birds, then sped away.

Julilly sat tense. Softly at first and then louder came the cry of baying dogs. Bloodhounds! Somehow their scent had been found and they or other slaves like them were being followed. Lester heard too. He shook Adam. Julilly called Liza.

"Pack everything in your bags." Lester spoke quickly. "Roll up your pants, and we'll walk north, straight through the middle of this stream. It will kill our scent."

11

The days and nights strung together for Julilly, Liza, Lester, and Adam like a looped rope without an end. When they heard dogs barking or saw men on horseback, they waded through the watersoaked land of the swamps. When the sun shone they fell exhausted in some dank shelter or beneath dry canebrakes and thorn-covered thickets. Their clothes were torn and dirty, their feet were scarred and blistered with insect bites and they were always hungry. One day they found only pecans and hickory nuts to eat.

When it was safe and there was time, Adam and Julilly hunted for swamp rabbits and fished for catfish. Liza kindled small fires with flint and spunk that Massa Ross had given her. Lester charted their course. He studied the stars on clear nights and when it rained and there were clouds, he felt for moss that grew on the north side of the forest trees.

"How we gonna know when we've reached Tennessee?"

Julilly asked one night as they talked of Massa Ross and how much they needed him.

"I can read." Lester spoke bluntly.

"No slave I ever heard of was allowed to read. You is just tellin' a lie, Lester." Liza gave him a dark look and lapsed into one of her sullen moods. "One time my daddy bought himself a spellin' book with some money he saved from sellin' apples. You know what happened when the Massa found him lookin' at that book?"

Julilly didn't want to ask. She knew the answer.

Liza went on. "Massa grabbed that book and threw it in an open fire. Then he said, 'No nigger of mine is goin' to get uppity and try to read.' He tied my daddy's hands to a tree and stripped him to the waist. Then he got his whip and gave him fifty lashes. I had to watch. His blood ran all over the ground. I loved my daddy."

"It's no lie. I can read." Lester stood up and turned away from the three doubtful faces. "On the Hensen Plantation, one of the house slaves could read and Massa Hensen knew. He taught me to read and the Massa knew that too. He just made us promise never to tell anybody— not even Missy Hensen."

They sat for a moment on a dry log near the muddy banks of the Mississippi. They ate cold fish which had been cooked before sundown.

"Soon we'll cross into Tennessee," Lester said. "I'll see a sign beside the river when we get there, Massa Ross said.

Then we wait until night—maybe two nights. Massa Ross will come with a cart on the nearest road. We listen for three calls of the whippoorwill and then we meet him."

"He might not come." Adam spoke gently. Usually he was silent. When he did speak, the others listened carefully.

"Why you say that, Adam?" Julilly asked.

"Adam's right." Lester answered quickly. "He might not come. If something happens to him, he promised to send another man."

"How we gonna trust a man we've never seen before?" Liza was bent over, resting her head on her knees. She was too tired to look up.

"There's a password," Adam said again very softly. "We say to this man who gives the bird call, 'Friends with a friend.' He answers the same thing and then we trust him."

"Friends with a friend." Julilly repeated the password to herself over and over again. A mean, hateful man would never make up such words, she decided. She would trust whoever said it.

"I don't trust no white man," Liza muttered to herself.

The stars were bright that night and there were only the night sounds of lapping water, croaking frogs, and the hollow, chilling hoot of an owl. They walked near the river.

Julilly locked Liza's arm through hers. She could bear her friend's weight as well as her own. The long night walks were making her legs stronger. But Liza grew thinner and weaker. Lester, especially, was uneasy with her.

"Lester won't slow down for nobody." Julilly knew this in her heart. "Lester will fight and protect us from slave catchers, but he won't slow down."

Julilly listened to the plodding steps of gentle Adam behind her. "Adam and I will carry her if she gets more sickly," Julilly reassured herself and walked steadily forward along the path that Lester made for them.

It was still dark when the four of them came at last to a sign printed on a large high board beside the river. Lester read aloud—tennessee.

They stopped beside it. The open road settled far enough into the canebrakes, so that anyone passing by would never guess they were there. Two men on horseback galloped by, one on either side of the road. The moonlight outlined their figures. One of them was fat and carried a whip; the other one had a gun.

The four slaves sat immobile as stunned rabbits until the sound of hoof-beats disappeared. Adam was the first to speak.

"That fat man sure did look like Sims."

"He could be Sims," Lester agreed. "The way he beat his horse and waved his whip made me wonder."

"We'd best stay right where we are for a long time," Liza cautioned.

Julilly heard another noise. It was the clatter of wagon wheels. It might be Massa Ross. If the fat man was Sims and he turned around and rode back, he would recognize him! The four of them shared the same thought without speaking it. They moved farther back into the canebrakes.

The wagon came closer. When it reached the Tennessee sign, it stopped. There was silence. Then, three soft calls of the whippoorwill filled the air. It was their signal; but they had to be certain with the possibility of Sims so near.

Julilly knew at once what she had to do.

"Listen," she whispered to the others, "if it's somebody trickin' us from the Riley plantation, they'd right away know Lester and Adam and maybe Liza with her bent-up back. They wouldn't know me. I'm just a big, tall nigger boy the way I'm dressed now. I'll go first."

Lester hesitated, then nodded his approval.

Julilly took a deep breath like she was going to jump into the Mississippi River, and walked into the open.

She stood at the edge of the road and spoke hoarsely.

"Who is you?" Her voice quivered. She couldn't risk revealing the password.

"Friends with a friend," the man on the wagon answered. It wasn't Massa Ross, but this man knew the right password. Liza, Lester, and Adam came from the shadows. The man relaxed the reins and leaned over the side to see them better. He was brisk and small. It was hard to see his head because a wide-brimmed hat covered most of it. His lips smiled kindly above a white looped-over collar.

"You are the friends of Mr. Ross," he said simply. "The good man has been put in prison in Columbus, Mississippi, and we pray no harm will come to him. I've been sent in his place."

"Oh, Lord, help him," Liza prayed aloud.

"Massa," Lester interrupted, "two slave-hunters just passed by this way goin' north. We think they are from our place—the Riley plantation."

"Then we must hide you at once and talk later." The little man jumped to the ground. He threw back a large canvas that covered the wagon. Underneath was a thick layer of fresh straw.

"You must crawl under the straw toward the centre." He spoke swiftly like someone familiar with his task. "Then I will cover you with the canvas. If we are stopped, remain silent. I will do the talking." The kindly smile remained on his lips.

Julilly and Liza crawled in first and lay close together. Lester and Adam followed. It became pitch black when the little driver pulled the canvas over them.

"I can't see your face," Liza whispered.

Julilly didn't answer. She was grateful that Liza was there. She wondered about the small man who drove the wagon. Was he one of the Quaker Abolitionists? Would the slave holders catch him too and put him in jail with Massa Ross?

"Don't talk at all," Lester cautioned all of them.

The wagon jogged along the road. The straw was soft and sweet smelling, but Julilly's stomach ached with hunger. There had been no time that night to hunt for food. Even if the little man had bread for them, they couldn't stop now to eat it.

The rocking wagon and the soft hay tempted Julilly to sleep, but hunger kept her awake, even though her tired legs and arms felt like they were sleeping separate from the rest of her.

The clopping sound of men on horseback and a sudden jolt of the wagon unsettled the four fugitives. Lester whispered,

"Don't move even if the canvas is pulled back. If they find us, jump over the side of the wagon and run for the woods. They won't shoot with their guns, they want us alive!"

Julilly and Liza locked their arms together.

A loud, harsh voice called out.

"You Quaker Abolitionist, pull your wagon over by the side of the road. We're huntin' this road for runaway slaves from the Riley plantation. We figure this is the way they'd be comin' toward the North."

The voice didn't belong to Sims. Julilly said a grateful prayer for this. But it was someone sent by Sims and he was looking for the four of them.

"The devil with you Quakers and your wide-brimmed hats. Nigger lovers, that's what you are, the whole parcel of you." The gruff voice came closer.

There was the scuffling sound of two horses. Julilly knew it was the two men they had seen moments before.

"What do you want of me?" the small driver of the wagon asked clearly in a strong voice.

"We want to know if you've seen four slaves—two men and two girls—along this road tonight?"

"No." The Quaker didn't hesitate. "I haven't seen two men and two girls anyplace along this road."

It's a lie he's tellin', Julilly thought, and then checked herself. He wasn't lying, he had seen two men and two boys running out of the woods. That's what he thought he had in his wagon. Mr. Ross was a smart man to have them dress in boys' clothes.

"I don't trust one word you stealin' Abolitionists say." The man on the horse began talking louder. "Did you know that the new Fugitive Slave Act, just passed by Congress, lets the slave owners retake human property in any state—north or south."

"I am well aware of this cruel and unjust act," the wagon driver replied quietly.

"Unjust, you say." Now the slave catcher was shouting. "People like you can be put in jail and fined $1,000 for just givin' a fugitive a meal."

Julilly shuddered. How could they ever escape? They could even be hunted now in the free states of the North.

"We better see what this farmer has in his wagon." The other horseman finally spoke. "Get down and turn back the canvas on that wagon!"

Julilly heard their driver jump from his seat to the ground.

"You can see that it's hay I carry to my cousin in the next town." The Quaker continued to speak softly as he slowly pulled back the canvas from a corner of the wagon.

Julilly gripped Liza's arm. She didn't move, but she did open her eyes. Praise the Lord, it was still dark!

"It is hay." The second horseman spoke quickly. "We'd better be ridin' back to the river before daylight breaks. Those niggers hide themselves in the daylight."

They rode away without another word.

The little driver pulled the canvas back over the wagon. He leaned over it.

"When daylight breaks," he said to the four slaves who lay tense and shaken under the hay, "we'll stop in a deserted barn along the way and have our breakfast."

12

Daylight peeled away the shelter of darkness.

"This cart is a movin' trap," Liza finally said to Julilly. The cart jogged faster, throwing them forward and backward with each bump in the road.

Now that the day had come, noises surrounded them—horses' hoofs, clattering carts, talking people. This nearness to danger pressed against the slaves. It was suffocating, like the dryness of the hay and the dryness in their throats.

"I needs a long drink of water," Adam muttered from the far end of the wagon.

"You just forget water," Lester hissed crossly. "Hear those dogs barkin'. The slave catchers have them sniffin' along our tracks. If we weren't above the ground, joggin' along in this old wagon, they'd be bitin' at our heels right now."

Julilly listened. Far away there were high-pitched animal howls just as Lester said. Hunting dogs let loose on a man's scent couldn't be stopped any more than a bumble bee swarming over the sweetness of a blooming magnolia tree. Julilly knew this.

Suddenly the cart slowed its speed. It swerved abruptly onto a rougher lane which they could tell was narrow because tree branches scraped against the wagon's sides. The wheels splashed through shallow water, and then the wagon stopped.

There was need for speed because the little driver jumped from his seat and ripped the canvas from the cart.

"You must all come out of the hay at once," he said, "and hide inside the barn here." His voice was urgent.

Julilly stood up, brushing the hay from her hair and face. The freshness of the air and the brilliance of the sun were sudden joys she could not conceal.

"Liza, oh look!" she cried.

A swift moving stream sparkled beneath them. An old barn snuggled near by in a tangle of vines and gnarled tree limbs. It seemed to be waiting for them with an open door.

"My ol' body just won't untangle." Liza sat twisted in the hay.

Julilly bent down and lifted her friend from the wagon. It was no effort at all. She could carry Liza! Lester wouldn't have to worry about anybody slowing them down again.

"I seem to be growin' strong as a horse," Julilly laughed.

"I'm shrunk up poorly as a dried cricket," Liza scowled.

They joined Lester and Adam beside the stream and the four of them drank greedily.

The little Quaker paced nervously beside them.

"You must come inside the barn." His voice remained gentle but firm. "I must be on my way soon. If we are tracked down here there is no way I can protect you."

They followed him inside the barn. It was sweet smelling and dry. Someone had covered the floor with new-mown hay. They had made it ready for them. There was a bundle of food near the door.

The little driver drew all of them close to him beside an open window. He placed a round glass object on the flat window-sill. A black needle quivered inside it. He showed them how the needle always pointed north—the same as the North Star.

"I am leaving this compass with you," he explained and he chipped it slightly with his knife a little east of north. "You must not go straight north, it is too dangerous. Follow the needle east until you come to the Cumberland Mountains near the city of Knoxville. In the mountains there are caves for shelter and Indian paths to guide you."

The fugitives listened carefully. Julilly repeated the strange names over and over in her mind.

The little man pushed his wide-brimmed hat back from the shadows of his face. For the first time Julilly noticed his bushy grey eyebrows and deep-set kindly eyes. He talked about mountain ranges they would cross and cities they would come to. He believed they were going to get to Canada. All four of them needed this faith in their venture. They drew closer to him, more hopeful than they had been since leaving Massa Ross. The kindly man looked into the faces of each of them, as they stood quiet and expectant around him.

"I just wish I could take you right to the border of Canada." There was unexpected fervour in his voice. "Slavery is a horrible evil."

He pulled a round, sturdy watch from his pocket—then checked the position of the sun in the sky. He became nervous again and spoke quickly.

"The mountains will take you into Kentucky to the city of Lexington," he said. "Here you can follow the railroad tracks by night. They lead straight north to the city of Cincinnati in Ohio to the home of Levi Coffin. Don't forget his name. He is the 'president' of the Underground Railway."

The Underground Railway? Julilly was puzzled. Had these Abolitionists built a road under the ground that led all the way to Canada? She would have to remember to ask Massa Levi Coffin about this.

"God bless each of you," the little Quaker called as he ran to his wagon.

The four slaves watched him leave. He had given them

hope and a safe place to stay. His cart of hay bumped up and down on the small, deserted road.

THE FOUR OF THEM felt almost gay as Lester opened the bundle of food. Bread, cheese, and dried venison lay before them. A ray of sun from the broken window spread over it with golden warmth. Lester gave each of them a portion and tied the remainder inside the bundle again. They walked about the barn swinging their arms and legs. For one day and one night this barn was their home. It had walls and a roof. And a blessed flow of fresh water ran before their door.

"A gift, straight from the Lord," Liza declared.

"No hound dog is gonna sniff our scent over this rushin' water," Adam laughed.

Adam found an old pail. He turned it over and began beating a small rhythm with a stick. Julilly caught the swing of a song in it and began to dance. Liza didn't smile, but she clapped her hands, swaying back and forth with the rhythm. Lester, sitting in a corner, was thoughtful but not displeased.

"Before the sun sets we should catch some fish," Adam said, laying down his pail and walking to the door. Lester joined him.

"We'll go across the stream, where the trees are thick," he said. "Nobody can see us there."

"It would be safer if you didn't cross the stream,"

Julilly called out to them. But they didn't hear. They were already splashing through the water.

Julilly watched the gold sheet of sun stretch across the barn wall. The fresh hay felt soft against her feet. She thought of washing her clothes in the flowing stream and laying them in the sheet of sun to dry.

"If you've got to wear rags"—Julilly could hear Mammy Sally's voice singing these words way back at Massa Hensen's place—"keep them clean."

There was quiet when the men left. Julilly and Liza pushed the hay into a corner.

"We've got a bed," they laughed together.

They found a board and propped it on some logs to make a table. They put the bundle of food carefully beneath it.

"We've got us a house fit for a fine Missy." They sang the words together.

The rushing stream swallowed the man noises of the road. Only the clear song of a mockingbird could be heard above its rippling. Even the wind, playing through the leaves, was quiet. There was no crackle of branches to tell where Lester and Adam had gone.

It didn't seem real when the yelping noise of hound dogs entered the safety of the sun-drenched barn, shooting through the air like an arrow. Julilly cried out against it. She and Liza grabbed the bundle of food and the compass from the window ledge. They crawled into a

far corner of the barn and began scratching at the hay to pull it around them.

The yelping came to the edge of the stream. There were scuffs and pounding of horses' hoofs. The mockingbird flew away, leaving the sky for a moment empty of its song. But the emptiness filled with the cries and shouts of men and of whips cracking into the playful leaves.

Julilly sobbed. Liza's sore back tightened. A cloud erased the sheet of sun.

The hound dogs splashed into the water. They mixed lapping water with nervous yelping. Their swinging noses sniffed the scent of Adam and Lester and they bounded, screeching up the river into the grove of trees. They crashed through the bushes. The horses stamped behind them, and the men shouted from their saddles, their whips ripping the air.

Low cries of pain and terror rose from up the stream. Julilly and Liza stood helpless in the doorway of the barn, wringing their hands. The cries were from Lester and Adam. The dog sounds now were growls and snapping.

"They've been caught," Liza moaned, rocking crazily back and forth.

Julilly felt dark, as if night had fallen and closed around them and they were trapped with no escape. The dogs began to whine. They had found their prey. But the shouting, men-sounds didn't stop. Nor did the moaning, pleading slave-sounds. And, winding through them all, binding them horribly together, were the clanking sounds of chains.

Julilly wept. Tall, proud Lester in chains again; kind, simple Adam groaning beneath a cracking whip . . .

"Grab the food and the compass, Julilly, and get your bundle." Liza's voice was harsh and rasping. "The sounds are gettin' closer. They is comin' to this barn."

Julilly jumped up and gathered their meagre supplies. Together they watched the quivering arrow on the compass point to the east. They knocked the table apart, kicked the straw about the floor, then ran up the stream in the opposite direction to kill their scent. They left it finally to enter a grove of trees across the main road. They headed east into denser undergrowth, then stopped.

"There's no more pretendin' on this trip, Liza." Julilly hunched beneath a shrub. Her face was grim. The line of her mouth was rigid. "It'll take a load of hard work, plain luck, and lots of prayin' to get us both to Canada."

Liza faced the North. Her fists tightened. "Lester's that determined for freedom, he'll break those chains and drag Adam right along behind him."

They huddled together, listening to the disappearing yelps of the hound dogs.

13

It wasn't until the night closed over them that Julilly and Liza felt safe to begin their journey east toward the mountains. "The Appalachians," the Quaker-man had called them. They ate a scant portion of their food. It had to last for at least one more day. They found a handful of berries on a bush beside their hideout and the sweet juice quenched their thirst. It was the one bright happening in a grim day of fear and despair over the capture of Lester and Adam.

A large moon lit the sky, exposing all the open paths and roads. The girls stayed among the trees and bushes, remembering the cruel riders of the night before. Because of the moonlight, it was possible to see the compass, and they checked it often to be certain their course was true.

Their feet hurt, their legs and arms were scratched, but they pushed themselves on through the tangled paths and jagged rocks almost beyond endurance. Near dawn, they stopped by a shallow stream to drink and wash, allowing themselves only a little of the dried venison and stale bread. They ate slowly and silently, saving their words as though savouring the one thing left that they could use freely and abundantly.

"We got to find a good place to hide for the day," Julilly said dully. She stood up slowly and pulled Liza up with her hand. They walked on. An overgrown path led through the rocks and trees.

"Every step's goin' up," Liza breathed heavily. "We must have reached the mountains." She climbed, bent and haggard, on her hands and knees.

The morning mist that spread around them parted and dispersed. Far below they could see a few small farms. The animals and people moved about like tiny ants.

"These are the mountains for sure." Julilly leaned exhausted against a tree, but at least she could stand upright. She worried about Liza.

"From now on we travel north," she said. They both leaned over the compass and found the little arrow pointing straight ahead of them.

A large rock jutted across the path and above it was a hole in the mountain's side.

"Round as the doorway of a snake," Liza exclaimed.

"Must be one of those caves the man told us about." Julilly started climbing toward it, and Liza joined her. They looked inside. The floor was dry and sandy, the walls around and above solid stone. They walked deeper inside and darkness closed over them like the canvas on the Quaker-man's cart. Julilly stretched out her arms and she couldn't see her fingers.

"We'll sleep near the front of this hole," Julilly announced. They turned toward the opening. "You sleep first, Liza." Julilly leaned wearily against one of the rocks.

Small, wiry Liza dropped exhausted into a curl around the food bundle. She had spent all the strength her ill-used body could muster. Julilly bent over her little crippled friend. Now that Lester was gone, she would have to be the one to decide which way they should go. Liza could do no more than just keep her aching body moving. She'd have to worry about food, too. There didn't seem to be anything to eat on these craggy mountains.

The pink spread of sunrise came. It covered Julilly and turned her ragged shirt to gold. All was peaceful, as far as she could see. She breathed deeply of the morning fragrance and forgot that she was hungry. The sun rolled itself bit by bit onto the earth and spread out its warmth. It touched Julilly, brushing the cold earth from her feet and drying the dampness of her ragged shirt. She felt herself melting into a warm pool of light, soft and protecting. Julilly closed her eyes and went to sleep.

The two girls slept through the noonday sun. They slept while a deer crossed before the doorway of their cave. Its delicate nose sniffed the grass near by. Its timid eyes caressed them, and moved on.

In the early afternoon a soft grey mockingbird flew from the sky onto the white-barked branch of an aspen. It preened among the shimmering, sunflecked leaves, before bursting into a loud clear song.

Liza and Julilly stirred. The clear song brought a memory of Mississippi.

"It's mornin' and cotton pickin' time and I've slept too long . . ." Julilly jumped to her feet, hitting her head on the rock ledge above her. Liza lifted herself up slowly. There was pain in every bone she moved.

"Looks like I should have been on watch by now," Liza sighed, relieved that Julilly was still beside her and that only a mockingbird had found their hide-out.

"I've been sleepin' too, Liza." Julilly felt guilty and troubled. She had vowed that she would take every precaution while watching and hiding from slave catchers.

But there were no accusations from Liza. She reached for the food bundle, and turned it carefully inside out. A few crumbs and a small piece of bread no bigger than a bird's egg was all she found inside. She broke the bread and divided the dry crumbs. Julilly hunted for a spring and filled her gourd with water. They nibbled the bread and drank great gulps of water, but were still hungry. They would have to find more food. They couldn't climb all night over the mountains without eating. Julilly walked about the outer rim of the cave looking for berries or even roots that they could chew. There was nothing.

"We can't walk, Liza, 'less we get some strength from eatin'," Julilly said.

"We can't just sit here, Julilly, and waste away." Liza's voice was hard and determined. She was looking down into the valley where scattered farmhouses sent up spirals of smoke like cobweb clouds—smoke from cooking food.

Ahead of them stretched the peaks of the Appalachian mountains marking the direction north that they must take. The mountains meant days of rocky climbs up and down steep Indian trails. They meant plants, and animals, and trees, and rushing water that was new to the slave girls from the flat lands of the cotton-growing South.

Julilly looked at her friend and then at the valley farms below.

"I guess we know, Liza, what we got to do. We got to travel on and when dusk comes, we got to walk down to one of those houses, use some of the money Massa Ross gave us, and buy some food." Julilly felt for the crumpled dollar bills in the bottom of her bundle.

"That's what we got to do," Liza nodded.

They sat silently for a long time but there was nothing else to say. They picked up their meagre bundles and the compass and began climbing slowly down the side of the mountain.

The path they took led to a small clearing, surrounded by thick bush and a few tall pines. In the centre of it stood a square log cabin. It was sturdy and warm and lived-in because smoke spiralled softly from its chimney.

"This is where I got to go, Liza." Julilly took a deep breath and clutched one of the dollar bills in her hand. She quickly smoothed down her hair. It was the first time since the journey began that she had even thought how she must look. The short haircut was growing and her hair was bristly and unkempt.

"You stay here, Liza, in case we got to run."

Liza said nothing, but rubbed her thin, scarred legs and nodded.

Julilly walked forward. She kept her eyes on the cabin door, knowing that she mustn't stop until she got there. As she walked closer she could smell cooking food and her need for it grew so desperate that she ran to the door and knocked loudly.

For a moment there was no answer and then the door swung open widely and a gaunt, white farm woman stood tall and defiant in front of her. She held a gun and pointed it straight at Julilly. There was no fear on her stern, weathered face. She was as sturdy and strong as her cabin, and her dress was thick and woollen and had no holes.

The nearness of the cooking wiped all caution from Julilly's mind. She held out her money, trying to look around the gun and see inside the cabin.

"I got money," Julilly said. "I want to buy some food."

The woman stood still. Her lips barely moved, but the voice that came through them was a loud, clear whine. Her words could have been bullets from the pointed gun.

"You get off my land, you nigger slave." The words whined through the clearing and into the still, silent woods.

"You've been running away and you've been stealing money." She whined evenly without a quiver of fear.

Julilly crumpled the money inside her fist.

"Now get off my land, and get off fast"—the woman still didn't move her lips—"or I'll use this gun, and I've got a right good aim."

Julilly turned around and ran. She stumbled into the tangle of bushes looking frantically for Liza. A bony arm grabbed her leg. It was Liza.

"Come back here," Liza whispered, "there's a cave."

This time Liza led Julilly. The cave was small but sheltered by dead trunks of fallen trees. They huddled beside each other, shaking and frightened.

"That woman looked mean as a one-eyed crow, aimin' that gun at you," said Liza finally.

Julilly laughed a little and jammed the money deep into her bundle. It was such a relief to be safe and to be with Liza.

"Well you sure is better company than an old cold gun." Julilly tried to smile.

But there was no returning humour from Liza.

"We've got to try again, Julilly, and this time it's my turn." Liza began crawling painfully from the cave. Julilly lifted her up by her arm and hunted for the path that had led them into the clearing. They both knew that food must be found soon or they would be too weak even to look for it.

They plodded slowly in the opposite direction and this time they came to a flat plateau with waving grass. Some cows nibbled, their bodies swaying to and fro. A clear-sounding bell rang from the neck of one of them.

The cows were heavy with milk, but neither Julilly nor Liza had ever milked a cow or been near one. Julilly did remember Massa Hensen's herd coming home at dusk and following the leader, whose bell tinkled around her neck.

"We'll wait here a bit and when they start toward home, we'll follow them." Julilly sat on a smooth rock behind a thicket of low protecting brush. Liza joined her.

"It seems if a cow can fill itself with grass, we could do it too," Julilly mused, watching the friendly animals rip and munch great mouthfuls of green.

"We ain't cows." Liza frowned.

Julilly laughed. It burst forth unexpectedly, like a lid popping off a boiling pot. Bubbling inside her was a set of fears that sent a tingling prickle right to the ends of her fingers.

"I know we've got to do it, Liza"—Julilly spoke without looking at the sullen face of her friend—"but it means

101

talkin' to white folks again, beggin' them for somethin' to eat. They won't take our money. I'm scared."

"We can do it, Julilly. You got strength and you got courage. I've been askin' the Lord to give us help."

Strength and courage. Julilly thought about these words. That's what Mammy Sally had. It meant looking right at danger without bowing down your head. Like Lester did when the chains cut his ankles. It was hard, thinking of Lester. It brought fear and more pain. He had chains around him now and was bleeding on his ankles.

The girls sat close together. They whispered their plans. They would follow the cows to the farm house. If the farmers wouldn't give them something to eat they would have to take food—maybe corn from the fields. If the farmers caught one of them, the other one would creep into the house at nightfall and set her free.

The sweet-smelling grass rustled around them, for the cow with the bell swung her head back and forth near the rock where the girls sat. The girls didn't hear or see a tall, white-faced farmer standing directly behind them.

There was no time to hide or run when he walked around and faced them.

Liza grabbed Julilly's arm.

"Lord, save us," she cried.

Julilly stared at the farmer. Terror and fascination mixed inside her head.

This man was no Sims or Riley kind of farmer. He had a fresh, home-made look. There was nothing mean about his blue eyes and the straight, pale eyebrows on top of them.

He smiled.

"Slaves?" he asked.

The girls didn't move.

The farmer grabbed the collar of the belled cow and began walking down the mountain path. He waved for Liza and Julilly to follow.

It seemed the right thing to do. He hadn't touched them and he wasn't making them go. But they walked a safe distance behind him.

They turned around a grove of tall pine trees and came to another stretch of flat land. On this place, however, there were rows of small neat cabins. But not slave cabins. They weren't worn and shabby. They were new and shining with boxed-in gardens behind them and bright flowers growing around the edges. Women in long skirts moved about busy with their work; their light, pale hair pulled back tightly into tidy buns. Little children, covered with skirts and pants, skipped and sang and played with one another. They stopped only for seconds to stare at Julilly and Liza. It was a common sight, it seemed, for runaway slaves to follow a farmer into their village. There was no fuss at all.

One woman came forward, almost as if she were expecting them. She spoke to the farmer with strange words.

"We speak German," he said to the girls.

"German?" they repeated after him. The word had no meaning at all for Liza and Julilly, but they followed her. They walked into one of the bright new cabins. Turned inside out, it wouldn't matter, Julilly decided: all sides were scrubbed and polished.

In the kitchen, the biggest kettle the girls had ever seen sat on the floor steaming with warm, clean water.

The woman smiled. "Girls?" she said, and pointed to their ragged pants and shirts. The boys' clothes hadn't fooled her.

"You wash in tub." The English words came slowly for her. "You give old clothes to me." She handed them a square of soap and two white towels.

She waited. The girls peeled off their ragged, mud-soaked garments. They dipped their hands carefully into the water. The woman laughed.

"You get in there all the way and scrub. Hair too." She picked up their clothes with a stick and left the room.

Liza and Julilly looked at one another.

"You is the dirtiest girl I ever seen." Liza leaned toward Julilly. "You scrub me and I'll scrub you."

Julilly saw the scars from whippings criss-cross over Liza's back. She quickly looked away and climbed slowly

over the side of the tub. "I never put myself into no washtub before, but it feels mighty pleasant." She sank slowly into the water.

"I feels like a skinned catfish." Liza grinned and splashed down beside her friend.

The girls scrubbed their faces, their hair, their legs. Soapsuds hid the water. First it was white, then grey, then brown.

"Turnin' into the ol' Mississippi River," Julilly giggled.

They stepped outside the tub and dried themselves soft and smooth. Different women entered the kitchen. Two of them carried the tub outside to empty the water. Another slipped long, clean shirts over the girls. Another put food on the table—glasses of milk, thick bread, rich butter, slices of venison. Liza and Julilly sat on the benches and ate.

The women chatted in low voices—always in the strange German.

Then the first woman came in—the one who had taken their clothes. She shook a scolding finger at them.

"Eat slow," she said. "Some now—some after sleep."

She spread clean mats on the floor. They had the sweet smell of grass, from the meadows where the cows ate. There were no buzzing flies—no sick whine from mosquitoes—no need to hide in this clean, scrubbed cabin.

"My skin feel so clean, I think it must be shinin'." Julilly yawned.

Liza smoothed the white shirt over her knees, and slowly rubbed her hands together, turning them back and forth to view their cleanness. Two large tears rolled down her cheeks onto her lap. She wiped them away roughly.

"It's just that I've never been clean all over before," she tried to explain.

The woman who spoke a little English smiled. She took Julilly's hand and then Liza's hand and led them to the mats.

"Sleep," she said and walked away.

The gold sunlight, filtering through the open door, faded and faded and faded, until it was the half-light time before dark. The girls moved their mats close together and slept at once.

It was a long sleep for Julilly and Liza. Several times they jumped when early morning noises woke them. But they stretched their feet over the clean mats. They felt the safety of the farm cabin and slept some more.

"My tired bones are layin' here side by side feelin' good and happy," Liza smiled.

"I'm gonna sing," announced Julilly. At first it was a hum:

I am bound for the promised land
I am bound for the promised land

Then the song burst into full-throated singing in a

voice so like Mammy Sally's that Julilly wondered if it were hers.

Oh, who will come and go with me.
I am bound for the promised land

The women and children from the row of cabins came to the door and listened. They smiled. One of them shook her head and wept.

Two of the women came into the room, chattering German. More food was placed on the table and the girls ate. It wasn't until the woman who spoke English walked through the door carrying their washed and mended pants and shirts that Julilly and Liza knew their visit had ended.

The woman handed them the clothes and two bundles of food.

"You change clothes now and then go." She said the words slowly and with difficulty. "Slave hunters in the valley. Go high to the mountains—then north."

The girls scrambled into their clothes. They hooked the bundles of food over their arms.

"You Abolitionists?" Julilly asked, stumbling through the long word with great difficulty.

"No, Mennonites," the woman said. "This place we built away from people. It is Felsheim, Tennessee."

"It must be like a church," Liza explained to Julilly as

they started toward a thickly wooded area on the mountainside. "My daddy is a Baptist."

"God bless you," the woman called from the row of clean cabins in the green valley.

Julilly and Liza didn't know how to express their gratitude to this kind lady. They couldn't even talk about it to each other. Human kindness from the villagers of Felsheim had negated a little of the human cruelty that had made them slaves. It was hard to know how to accept these offerings from white folks.

14

There wasn't much danger from slave catchers on the high mountain paths at night. But even without them, this wild place was terrifying and strange for Julilly and Liza. High-pitched animal cries that they had never heard before echoed in and out of the tall black mountain peaks. Their path sometimes became "slim as the string bindin' a cotton bale," as Liza exclaimed.

The girls held onto one another and once Julilly had to grab a swaying tree limb to keep from slipping down the mountain's side. Liza fell against her, hanging to her waist. They climbed up again on their hands and knees.

"If that North Star wasn't up there steady, beckonin' to us," Julilly shuddered, "I couldn't go on."

Before long, a strange, nervous wind began to blow. It skittered about—twirling up the stones along the path— then jumping into the trees and making ugly, swaying brushes of the giant pines.

A cloud smashed across the moon and erased their

path. It was dark now, as dark as the deep end of a cave. The air began to chill. Julilly and Liza stopped climbing and held onto the trunk of the nearest tree. The wind lashed around them like a slave owner's whip.

Someplace near by there was a long, cracking noise and then a thud. When the flashes of lightning came, Julilly and Liza could see a giant tree, torn from the earth with its raw, useless roots exposed to the storm. Thunder pounded in the sky, and then rain swept down like moving, walls of water. Another flash of lightning. This time the girls saw a flat place close at hand, shielded by an overhanging rock.

"Get all the tree limbs you can find, Liza, and pile them under that rock," Julilly screamed above the wind.

The pile grew high. They dragged heavy limbs that could not blow away.

"Now we'll dig a place under this rock," Julilly screamed again.

They scraped and grovelled. Their hands bled; but a small shelter did take shape, big enough for the two of them to squeeze inside. They shoved their bundles ahead of them.

"It's dry in here." Liza rubbed her hands over the ground.

But their newly-patched clothes dripped with water, and they chilled each time the wind blew through their makeshift hovel. There was nothing to do but take their clothes off, wring the water from them as best they could, and hang them over branches that were still dry. They covered themselves with pine needles and bunches of dried leaves and dug deeper with sticks into the dry earth.

They lay down close to each other for warmth. Somehow they slept, and when they woke the wind had stopped blowing. Mountain birds chirped their early morning songs and a faintly pink sun spread shyly across the sky. The girls peered through their shelter of branches. Fallen limbs and scattered leaves criss-crossed over the ground.

"Looks like somebody stirred the whole place up with a big wooden spoon." Julilly pushed her head clear of the branch above her.

"Nobody is gonna come lookin' for runaway slaves in this mess." Liza shook the still damp clothes and hung them carefully over a limb in the warming air.

The sun rose. It was humid and hot. The damp clothes steamed, and then blew stiff and dry. Gratefully the girls dressed and ate a small amount of the food packed for them by the good women of Felsheim.

"We'd best walk in the daylight," Julilly said. "There's no paths left and no signs of people."

"Tryin' to step over all these sticks and stones when nighttime comes is more than my two legs can manage," Liza agreed.

They decided to stay near the covering trees at all times and take cover at once if any stir of life was heard around them. They trudged along whatever trails they could find. Sometimes furry little animals jumped across their path, but the wild beasts that howled in the night seemed to take cover for the day. The girls climbed on and on, only stopping for drinks from the flooded mountain streams. Their guide was the needle of the compass which never left Julilly's hand.

The land was getting flatter and flatter, and the protecting mountain peaks were behind them. That night they rested uneasily in a cornfield near a road.

In the very early morning, Julilly saw an old coloured man hobbling along the road, pulling a cart behind him. She crawled quickly from their hideout and walked up to him. She had no fear of this ancient white-haired, black-faced man.

"Can you tell me what town I'm comin' to next?" she asked.

The old man jumped a little. Julilly startled him. It seemed as if he had trudged this road a thousand times and never had a black girl bound out right in front of him before. He stopped his cart and looked at her carefully.

"Lexington, Kentucky," he answered kindly. Then he whispered, "You a slave? You runnin' away?"

Julilly didn't have to answer. The old man knew. He looked cautiously down the road behind him as though expecting someone. Then he pulled his cart to the side of the road and lowered the handles to the ground. He reached inside his loose jacket and drew out a half loaf of bread.

"This is for you, child," he said softly. His wise old eyes lighted on her briefly, then focused far away with tired patience.

"If I was a young man, I'd go 'long," he said. He peered again down the road. "Hide in those bushes, boy. When night comes follow the railroad tracks to Covington. There's a free coloured man named Jeb Brown lives there. He'll get you 'cross the Ohio River in his little boat. You've got to cross the Ohio to get to Canada."

Julilly was startled when she heard "Canada." How did the old man know? But she didn't question him. She held his hand instead and thanked him from her heart.

The old man's back was more bent than Liza's, she noticed. His shabby clothes barely covered it. But he had strong arms and steady feet and he had a pleased look on his face since giving Julilly the bread. He started toward his cart, when a man on horseback swerved around the corner of the road and stopped beside him.

Julilly ran quickly to the shelter of the cornfield.

The man on horseback pulled in the reins of his horse and glared down at the old man.

"What you mean, Joe," he cried out, "restin' by the road so early in the morning? Get along there." He twirled a whip in the air.

The old man leaned down and picked up the handles of his cart and plodded on down the road.

Julilly and Liza held each other and sobbed.

"He's a slave too," Julilly cried. "He'll be hungry today. He gave us all his food."

She held the bread gently in both her hands.

THE GIRLS HID FAR AWAY from the road during the long, hot day. Twice a train passed near by, clanging its bell and hissing its steam. The little compass always pointed north toward the sound. It wouldn't be hard to find the tracks when night came.

They nibbled on the old man's bread and tried some ears of uncooked corn, but there was no water and the food was hard and dry. Late in the afternoon some men came walking through the fields. Liza and Julilly lay flat on the ground. The men passed them by, walked toward the road, and disappeared.

"They gave me a good fright." Liza's hands shook as she lifted herself from the ground.

"I'd say we is havin' more good luck than bad on this day," Julilly answered gratefully.

Night came early, for clouds collected overhead and changed the sky into a slate-grey lid. The girls crept carefully toward the road and discovered that the silver tracks ran right along the side of it. Tonight it was good that the moon was covered; for there was nothing to hide behind on the open tracks.

The girls walked on the ties facing the north wind. The tracks cut through fields and forests and it seemed almost that they were silver ropes pulling them on and on and on to Canada.

Once during the darkest part of night, a train roared and chugged and hissed behind them. They stumbled off the tracks into an empty barn as the earth started to shake. There was hardly time for the girls to see the train before it passed—screeching far ahead of them.

Julilly felt its speed and thought how fast it could take them north—faster than a bird could fly or a horse run.

THE TRACKS WERE THEIR GUIDE on a second night. This time the North Star shone steadily above them, but Julilly and Liza were frightened and ill at ease. It was light as day. Anyone could see them striding thong the uncovered tracks. They crept down into a grove of trees, feeling hungry and tired: there had been nothing to eat since they finished the old man's bread. A field of corn waved in the night wind, its ears hung heavy with grain.

"We'll start us a fire and roast some of those ears," Julilly decided.

They were starting to gather dry sticks, when a dog came bounding and barking out of the field toward them. They ran for the nearest tree. Julilly lifted Liza up into the lowest branch and then swung herself up beside her. The dog circled and barked around the trunk. The girls were tense and their hearts pounded so fast it was hard to breathe. Could this be a sniffing old slave catcher's dog, they wondered.

Then they heard a sharp whistle. The dog stopped barking and began to whine. Footsteps crunched near by.

"What you chased into that tree, Pal?" a low-pitched voice asked eagerly. "Somethin' for us to eat?"

Liza and Julilly looked down. It was a black man!

"Joy and praise the Lord!" Julilly cried, loud enough for the man to hear.

"You hush, Julilly"—Liza grabbed her arm—"you trust people too soon."

But it was too late to be quiet now.

"You Jeb Brown?" Julilly called down to him.

The girls were silent. The man hadn't answered.

Finally he said, "No, I ain't Jeb Brown and I don't aim to get mixed up with him. It's a dangerous business he's in."

The girls climbed higher into the tree.

"Don't you be afraid of me," he called to them.

There was a long silence. Julilly and Liza were still tense and afraid.

"Now listen to me," the man said in a low voice. "You come down out of that tree when my dog and me leave. You walk straight ahead through those trees to the north until you hear the running water of the Ohio River. Then you look along the river bank till you see a little house with one candle lighted in the window. That's all I got to say."

The man whistled for his dog and together they crunched into the bush and off into the crackling leaves of a cornfield until there was no sound from them.

Julilly was the first to speak.

"That man's got no more courage than a mouse," she said. "Let's climb down from here now and find the real Jeb Brown."

They slid down the tree with Julilly keeping a firm grasp on Liza's arm.

It was easy to walk north through the grove of trees and then down a row through a cornfield where the leaves twisted with the wind like hundreds of waving arms.

At the end of the field they heard the steady splash of moving water.

"The Ohio River, Liza," Julilly whispered. "We've reached the Ohio River!"

They walked toward the sound, but stopped abruptly when they saw the flickering light of a single candle from the window of a small log cabin.

"That's the cabin of Jeb Brown," Julilly said and started toward it. Liza pulled her back.

"You believe everybody," she chided. "That man could be tellin' lies."

Julilly didn't listen, but dragged Liza with her toward the cabin. When they reached the door, Julilly rapped softly.

A dog growled inside. Then came a man's voice.

"Who's there?"

"A friend with friends." Julilly used the faithful password.

A door creaked open exposing a big, straight man with crinkly grey hair and coal-black skin. Beside him growled a large brown dog.

"You Jeb Brown?" Julilly asked.

"You is speakin' to the right man," he said, urging them inside.

"Quiet, Pal." He patted the dog's head and then called, "Ella, we got freight—two packages of dry goods."

A sprightly little brown-skinned woman stood there. Her eyes twinkled above the candle which she now carried in her hand. Her white hair was piled about like fresh-picked cotton.

Julilly looked quickly around the room. The cabin was orderly and clean. It could have been a cabin in Felsheim.

Jeb hurried about pulling down shades over all the windows. Ella walked behind a cupboard of dishes, motioning for the girls to follow. She pushed against the wall and it opened like a door! Ella and the girls slipped through, followed by Jeb, and the wall closed behind them.

"You stay out there, Pal," Jeb said to his dog, "and this time you bark as much as you want if you hear any noises."

The room behind the wall was small but cozy. There were mats on the floor and a long spread-out table with benches around it. The only window was above them, cut into the roof.

"Looks like you were expectin' us." Julilly now felt that she could speak out loud.

Liza slumped to the floor—too tired and hungry to walk another step.

"Poor child." Ella leaned over her. She looked closely at her face, then laughed. "I thought you two was girls. We've been lookin' for you since your friends Lester and Adam were here."

"Lester and Adam!"

"Now you two just rest on those mats," big, kindly Jeb said, settling himself on one of the benches. "I'll explain about everything, while Ella fixes us some supper."

There was no way the girls could rest now. They stood in front of Jeb demanding to know about Lester and Adam at once.

"Well, they came one night more than a week ago," Jeb said quietly. "Chains were hangin' from their wrists. They'd rubbed through the skin and both were bleeding."

Julilly closed her eyes wondering if she really wanted to know the rest of the story.

"Lester had a sprained arm. The big man, Adam, had a swollen foot—so sore he could hardly lift it."

"How'd they know to come here?" Julilly was awestruck that all of them should come to this lone cabin on the Ohio River.

"They came 'cause we're a station of the Underground Railway," Jeb answered simply. "Isn't that why you two came too?"

Ella interrupted by swinging through the secret door. Her arms held a tray with steaming food. She placed the lighted candle in the centre of the long table and around it spread a feast of fresh venison, warm corn bread, wild honey, milk, and butter.

They bowed their heads and Jeb prayed. It was a good prayer, full of hope and promise for the end of slavery.

"Amen," Liza added at the end of it with deep emotion.

It was so fine being here with coloured folks to talk with. Silently, Julilly thanked the Lord for this. Now, she and Liza could tell their names without being afraid; they could talk about the Riley plantation, and Mammy Sally, and Liza's preacher father. The white folks who'd helped them along the way were good and kind, but it wasn't the same. Jeb and Ella Brown were like having their own family sitting around.

Julilly and Liza filled their plates and Jeb told his story—how Lester and Adam had jumped from the slave catcher's wagon during the night they were captured, into a swamp, even though they were handcuffed together. For a whole night they stayed in the water to throw off their scent from the hunting dogs. They rubbed their chain against a jagged rock until it broke and they were free from each other. They drank swamp water and ate water cress. "Lester knew names of folks along the Underground Railway which he'd pledged to Massa Ross to keep secret—even from the two of you."

"Those boys were poorly and mighty sick." Ella interrupted. "I nursed them for a week in this very room. When they could walk, they left. They told us to watch for the two of you."

Julilly sat on her mat and cried. She had thought and dreamed of Lester and Adam dragging their heavy chains back to Mississippi. Now Jeb said they might be free right now in Canada. Inside her there was a welled-up fountain of joy. The tears came from its overflowing.

"But what's this Underground Railway?" Liza finally asked.

"You don't know 'bout the railway?" Jeb laughed. "The slave catchers gave us the name. They said runaway slaves just seem to disappear underground and that there must be a railway down there."

"We Abolitionists use the railway all the time," Ella laughed softly. "Coloured and white folks work together on it. Our homes, where we hide you slaves, are the 'railway stations.' The roads you all follow are the 'tracks.'

You runaway slaves are the 'freight.' The women are 'dry goods' and the men are 'hardware.'"

So that's why Jeb had announced them as packages of dry goods when they came to his cabin door. Julilly chuckled to herself.

"We aim to send you from here to the 'president' of the Underground Railway, Levi Coffin," said Ella. "He's a Quaker and he lives across the river in Cincinnati."

15

In the spare but sturdy cabin of Jeb and Ella Brown, beside the wide dark waters of the Ohio River, four people slept. But the dog, Pal, stirred restlessly. His black nose, pressed against the door, sniffed a people scent which was growing stronger. He rose and paced nervously to the bed of his master where he tugged at Jeb's sleeve.

Jeb woke instantly. He'd trained himself for this, and he'd trained Pal.

"Ella," he said softly, nudging his wife who slept beside him, "there's trouble comin'."

Ella rose at once. She made no sound, nor did she light her candle. The room was dark for the shades were still drawn, but she made her way quickly to the secret door and tiptoed to the mats where Julilly and Liza slept.

"Julilly—Liza." She shook them gently.

The girls sat up, alarmed and dizzy with trying to remember where they were. Ella calmed them with a steady hand on both of theirs.

"Pal smells people comin'," she whispered. "It could be slave hunters."

Julilly felt cold fear creeping over her, making her body stiff and almost immobile.

"Lord, help us again," she breathed.

"They ain't gonna catch us now when we've reached the Ohio River." Liza's whisper was fierce and determined. "We'll hide, or run, or even swim across that river, Julilly." Liza's look was one of bitter hatred.

"Listen to me." Ella Brown's voice remained calm and steady. She walked to the centre of the dark room and jerked at something swaying against the wall. A rope ladder fell down, leading up to the window in the roof.

"Roll up your mats and push them in the corner," she continued, giving her instructions in the same calm voice. "Take everything that belongs to you and climb up this ladder. Pull it up after you. Then close the window and lay flat on the roof. Nobody's been caught up there yet." She left the room.

The girls did exactly as they were told. Liza climbed up first because she needed Julilly behind to steady her. The roof was almost flat. They would have no trouble pressing against it, nor would they have any trouble hearing every sound inside the house.

People were arriving on horseback and Pal began barking wildly.

A voice boomed out of the darkness.

"Jeb Brown, you tie up that dog in there or I'll blow his head off . . ." This is Sheriff Starkey and a friend. We got a warrant and we aim to come in."

The girls shivered. They clung together and moved farther away from the window. Pal stopped barking and began to whine. The front door squeaked open.

"You free nigger slave stealers in there, light some candles or a lantern. You want us to break our necks in this black hole?" It was the booming voice of Sheriff Starkey.

Eventually the candles were lit. Liza and Julilly couldn't see.

The voice boomed on.

"My friend here," he shouted, "has come all the way from Vicksburg, Mississippi, huntin' four niggers who ran away from the Riley plantation. They're worth five hundred dollars apiece. That's a goodly amount, and we're aimin' to catch them alive."

"Sit down, Sheriff." The girls could hear Jeb's voice, low and unhurried. "Do you want Ella to fix you somethin' hot to drink?"

There was no answer. Just a shuffling and scraping noise as if furniture was being pushed and shoved around.

"If they're in here, we're gonna find them." The Sheriff was still shouting. "People say you got somethin' to do with that Underground Railway, Jeb. You just drop those nigger slaves into the ground and nobody ever sees them again."

There was still no answer from Jeb or Ella. Pal continued to whine softly.

The scuffling noises continued. Julilly wondered if they might be pulling up the floor boards to find the "Underground Train." What could she and Liza do against two strong men if they climbed onto the roof?

Liza seemed to read her mind.

"If they climbs onto this roof, we'll jump," she said. "We'll run to the river and hunt for Jeb's boat."

Julilly agreed.

At last it was quieter in the house below. The talk was low and the girls couldn't hear the words. Now and then there were hammer sounds as if one of the slave catchers might be trying to pound through a door.

Julilly hoped she wouldn't get dizzy or sick. She closed her eyes tightly, trying to shut out all the threats and poundings.

At last the front door banged open and the hard steps of two men could be heard clomping over the porch boards.

"We didn't catch you this time, Jeb," the Sheriff called from the back of his horse, "but we've got our eye on you. You hide any of those runaway niggers and we'll put you and Ella both in jail and fine you a thousand dollars."

There were no words from Jeb or Ella. The door closed and the clatter of horses' hoofs faded into the soft, black night.

Julilly and Liza climbed slowly down the rope ladder and back into the dark secret room.

Ella was already there. She drew the girls close to her.

"That sheriff," she murmured, "is a mean man. He's gone now, but he'll be back."

"Liza and I got to leave now," Julilly said. She stood tall beside the other two. "We can hide better in the fields."

Liza started to speak, then suddenly fell lifeless to the floor. She lay twisted and limp like a wilted plant whose stem had lost all means of sustenance.

Julilly bent down and shook her frantically.

"You can't just fade away from me now." Julilly became desperate. "I need you, Liza. I can carry you."

Frail, bent Liza lifted her head. Her fiery black eyes seemed separate from the fragile body around them.

"I'm comin', Julilly," she said fiercely. "I'm just restin' and I need a drink of Ella's hot soup."

Ella brought the warm broth immediately and held it to Liza's lips. It seemed to revive her, and she slowly stood on her feet.

"You need a good rest, child." Ella's voice filled with concern. "But it won't do to keep you longer. That sheriff is comin' back again tonight. I feel it in my bones."

Julilly shivered.

Ella went on, "Jeb figures to get you across the Ohio River tonight. Listen now, he's callin' to see if he gets an answer from the other side."

The girls listened. The eerie tremolo-call of the hoot owl drifted through the open window in the roof. There was a pause and then it came again and again. They waited. Three answering calls followed faint but clear, sounding like a faraway echo.

Ella was excited. "That hoot-owl call is the 'river signal.' It's lucky somebody's there tonight on the other side."

She moved quickly, gathering up the rope, then slipping through the secret door and untying Pal who was whimpering in a dark corner.

"You follow Pal and me to the river," Ella whispered to the girls. "Jeb's gonna row you across."

At the river's edge, Jeb was waiting in a small rowboat. It bobbed up and down on the ink-black water. Julilly searched for the opposite shore, but there was no end to the blackness. How would Jeb know where to go? Where would he steer this small bouncing skiff?

Jeb held the boat steady against the shore as the girls climbed in. Julilly steadied Liza and gave her the nearest seat. No one talked. There was just the sniffing sound of Pal and splash of moving water.

Jeb slipped onto the seat where the oars were anchored. He leaned toward Julilly and Liza and spoke softly. "Lean down, hold onto the sides and don't make no sound."

Ella shoved the boat into the water and waved good-bye.

"Ella and Jeb Brown are my friends forever," Julilly thought.

Jeb's oars dipped noiselessly into the black water. He gave mighty pulls with his strong arms. The boat must not flow with the current. It must cut across it. Julilly and Liza strained to help him. Three tremolo calls of the hoot owl trilled through the air. Jeb answered with a similar call, then turned the boat slightly upstream, responding to the "river signal."

For Julilly and Liza, the river held mystery and terror. They couldn't swim. There had never been time or a place to learn. They had never floated over a river in a boat before. Julilly felt the lapping water hit her hand. Sprays of water spun across her face.

Finally, the dim black outline of a shore appeared. A silent figure waved from the bank. Jeb threw him a rope and the boat was pulled silently ashore.

The man tugging at the rope was white. The girls noticed this at once. There was no greeting between the two men, just nods of recognition. But Jeb did grasp Julilly's hand and then Liza's. He didn't need to speak. The grasp was strong with warmth and courage.

"These helpin' hands is the rails and the engines of the Underground Railroad," Julilly thought to herself. "All the way from Mississippi to Canada they is pullin' and workin' and makin' a helpin' chain. There is some good people all across the land."

The girls were led quickly to a horse-drawn cart. A large drawer pulled out beneath it and they were tucked inside. The drawer closed. There wasn't room to move around, but there were warm, fresh-smelling blankets to lie upon.

"Well now I feels like I is really on a railway underground," Liza said quietly. There wasn't a sliver of light in any direction.

"We aren't supposed to see," Julilly chuckled. "Don't you remember, Liza, we is just two packages of dry goods." They needed to be light-hearted for a moment— to relax all the tight muscles that had held them frozen to Jeb and Ella Brown's roof and to allow Liza to recover from her sudden faintness.

The snug little drawer began jostling back and forth with the trotting of a horse and Julilly wanted to sing. Instead she thought the song inside her head—the way she had done long ago in the cabin at Massa Hensen's farm.

When Israel was in Egypt's land
Let my people go
Oppressed so hard, they could not stand.
Let my people go . . .

A low voice spoke softly through the boards above them.

"If all goes well, we'll reach the home of Levi Coffin in Cincinnati by morning. If we are stopped, don't make a sound."

16

Julilly and liza were asleep when the cart with the hidden drawer drew up to a large corner home on Broadway Street in Cincinnati. A chill drizzle swept over the lawn and across the long porch of the house, which circled a row of tall windows and a wide front door. It wasn't very light outside, but it was morning, and the leaves on the two spreading oak trees near the cart were shining green.

A sudden opening of the drawer brought chill and rain over the sleeping girls. They woke at once and crawled stiffly onto the street. Julilly held onto Liza, who found it hard to walk. The driver guided them to the door. He knocked three times and called softly, "A friend with friends."

The door opened at once.

Standing there to greet them was the tallest man Julilly and Liza had ever seen. His face was gaunt, as if he had sucked his cheeks inside his mouth. His blue eyes lifted them both up straight. There was no way not to look at them. They sought first Julilly's face and then Liza's, seeming to smile and weep and welcome them all at once. And above the blue eyes was a wide-brimmed Quaker hat.

The tall man swept them all inside.

"You have brought us some valuable-looking passengers this time," he said to the shivering driver of the cart, who was covered with a cloak that hid almost every part of him.

"Now you may switch off, put your locomotive in my stable and let it blow off steam." The tall man laughed a little as he gave the directions. "We will water and feed it."

"Thank you, Friend Coffin," the driver said and walked out of the door.

Levi Coffin, Julilly realized, the "president" of the Underground Railway.

Tall Mr. Coffin called toward another room.

"I think we've got dry goods from Mississippi." His blue eyes twinkled now with more laughter.

A hearty woman's voice answered.

"Well, bring the two packages from Mississippi into the dining room."

A strong woman with a kindly face and dark-rimmed glasses met them. Her long grey dress and round white cap seemed to fit with the long coat and short knee breeches of her husband.

"Poor dears." She put her arm around both girls. "You are cold and badly dressed."

From a stool near by she grabbed some shawls and covered each of them. She led them to chairs around a long dining-room table.

Julilly and Liza were startled. Four other black faces looked up at them, frightened faces with the look of rabbits caught in traps. Their hands were scratched, their hair matted; their clothes were muddy rags.

In a moment of quick anguish, Julilly knew that she and Liza looked like them. They did not smile or say where they came from. There was just a grateful silence of acceptance.

"Aunt Katie," a young voice called from the kitchen. "You can come now for the food."

Julilly and Liza ate quickly. There was warm porridge in a bowl and hot coffee in a white china cup for each of them. Julilly slid both hands around the smooth warm vessel. It thawed the aching cold from all her fingers and made them seem less rough and bruised.

As soon as the meal was finished, Aunt Katie and the girl from the kitchen whisked every dish from the table, and pushed all the chairs and benches back against the wall.

"This is done in case the slave hunters come. There is no need for them to become suspicious over a pile of dirty dishes." Aunt Katie smiled, then motioned for Julilly and Liza to follow her. The other slaves were sent with the kitchen girl.

Levi Coffin and the carriage driver could be heard entering the front door. But they weren't alone. A rough-voiced man was entering with them.

Julilly's heart jumped. He sounded like the sheriff from Jeb and Ella Brown's house.

"I know you are a respected store keeper in Cincinnati, Mr. Coffin, and a well-known Quaker"—the rough voice started softly but began getting louder—"but you are also known as the most notorious nigger thief in the whole state of Ohio."

There was no answer from Mr. Coffin.

Aunt Katie grabbed Liza and Julilly by the hands and led them into the nearest bedroom. She threw back all the bedding.

"Now I want you two to lie close together between the straw tick and the feather tick. I'll puff them up to give you room to breathe."

Julilly and Liza scrambled into the bed.

"You both lie quietly while I make up the bed," Aunt Katie said calmly. "I'll smooth the counterpane and put on the pillows." She paused. "You would never guess two people were tucked away inside."

The girls could hear the creaking of a rocking chair.

"I will pray for thee." Aunt Katie's voice was firm and

steady. "And don't you worry. Levi has no fear of the searchers. We seldom lose a slave to them."

The slave catcher with a voice like Sheriff Starkey could be heard from the dining room.

"Four valuable slaves have escaped from the Riley plantation in Mississippi." The searcher's voice was angry now. "The owner wants them back and he's offered a good price. I've been following them and my trail comes right to this house." He paused. "Why does a respectable man like you get mixed up in this devilish business, Coffin? I've got a legal warrant to search these premises."

The low, deep voice of Levi Coffin answered calmly and almost gently.

"My good man," he said, "I never conceal my opinions and I try not to give offence. But this you must know: at all times I obey the commands of the Bible and the dictates of humanity in feeding the hungry and clothing the naked and aiding the oppressed. And the good book mentions no distinction of colour in the doing of these deeds."

Julilly could hear each word. She listened carefully. Mister Coffin was saying that the Bible didn't care about the colour of people. If they needed clothes and food, you gave it to them.

There was a long period of silence and then a knock at the bedroom door. The kindly voice of Levi Coffin was formal as he pushed the door open and said, "Sheriff, this is where my wife reads and sews in the early morning hours . . . Catherine, Sheriff Donnelly seems determined to search our house."

Julilly held her breath. She felt that if she moved even a finger the sheriff might see. What if Liza coughed? Her skin felt damp and cold.

"Good morning, Sheriff. It's too bad you must be out in such stormy weather. Perhaps I should come to the kitchen and warm you some coffee." Aunt Katie spoke sweetly.

The sheriff sounded embarrassed. He stuttered. "It wa-wasn't my intention to dis-dis-disturb a lady in her bedroom."

The two men left the room, closing the door behind them. Their voices became a mumble.

Aunt Katie's rocker ceased squeaking. Julilly and Liza barely breathed. They were waiting for the large front door to open and close.

When it did, and before Aunt Katie could turn the coverlets back from the bed, Levi Coffin entered the bedroom again. He was breathless and his calmness was noticeably shaken.

"The sheriff has gone, Catherine, but I feel certain he will be back soon with more men for a thorough search of our house. I think it best that we dress all the slaves warmly and put them on the noon freight train for Cleveland."

"You are right, Levi." Aunt Katie's voice was no longer sweet, but hearty and practical once more. Her husband hastened down the hallway to warn the other slaves.

"You may come out now, girls." Aunt Katie whisked the coverlets to the bottom of the bed. "The boys' clothes are a good disguise, but they didn't fool me."

The girls scrambled from the bed, tangling their feet in the soft, clean-smelling blankets.

"I know you have had a good scare," she said, "and so have I." She walked to the near-by window and pulled the curtains apart.

"This dark grey day is on our side. Levi is right; we must get you both into Canada as quickly as possible."

Julilly and Liza stood quietly together in the centre of the neat, homey room. They felt like two leaves blown in from the rough winds of the field and forests. They were frightened and bewildered. Would the Lord keep protecting them from the slave hunters that followed them everywhere? How would they ever manage without all these brave people who kept helping them? Where was Levi Coffin sending them? Would the Underground Railway this time be a real train? Would they ever get to Canada?

"We keep movin'." Julilly broke the silence among them. "We keep bein' lifted up and put on board. Massa Ross started it way back there in Mississippi."

"Bless you, my children." Aunt Katie's eyes were misty

with tears. "I wish you could stay longer with me but there isn't time."

She took them to a small room with basins of hot water, bars of soap, and thick white towels. She instructed them to wash and to put all their dirty clothes into a basket.

"The sewing circle of our Quaker Meeting makes large supplies of clothes for all of you who stop at the Coffin 'depot.'"

Aunt Katie laughed. New clothes for Julilly and Liza were taken from a closet. "I think we'll keep you dressed as boys since the everlasting slave hunters are looking for two girls. I'll give you each a heavy sweater. You'll need them for the coming winter."

Julilly held the new clothes in her hands. The sweaters were knitted with warm yarn. They were the colour of the blue wisteria that hung lush and fragrant over Massa Riley's summer house in Mississippi. The yarn felt springy and was not worn smooth. She could hardly believe that when she was clean she was going to wear this beautiful sweater.

Liza grinned. "In such fine feathers, Lester and Adam will think we is Queen Victoria herself when we step on the land of Canada."

Liza gave Julilly a radiant smile. Julilly stared at her. Where was the old Liza? Where was bent, sullen, angry Liza now?

17

In their new sweaters with knitted caps that matched, Julilly and Liza were put inside a black, horse-drawn carriage which had been waiting on the street before the large Coffin home. Black curtains hung about its windows as though a death were being hidden someplace inside.

Aunt Katie clasped both girls in her arms. Levi Coffin searched their faces. His blue eyes glowed, warm and steady as the light from a pine-knot ember.

"God bless you both," he said, and closed the carriage door.

The girls were alone inside. Perhaps the other slaves had gone ahead or were waiting in another hiding place.

Julilly and Liza sat close together—looking like strangers to each other even in the closeted light. Julilly had never felt the warmth of new clothes. They hugged against her. It was pleasant and she smiled. She and Liza didn't look like slaves now. Would anyone know them, even if the door were flung wide open and mean old Sims stood scowling right before them?

Rain pattered against the carriage top. The wheels sloshed through puddles, but the rain was welcome. It was a curtain of protection.

"I feels safe and strong again, Julilly." Liza hummed the words. "And I feels like a fine, cleaned-up lady."

Julilly squeezed her hand. The carriage jolted steadily through the streets and the girls jolted with it side by side.

It was a short trip, for the driver could be heard calling to his horse, and the carriage began to skid as he pulled in the reins.

They heard what must be their driver talking to another man.

"A friend with friends," he said.

"And what do you want sent by freight?" another man asked.

"Two packages of dry goods," was the answer. "Drive to the end of the train station and we'll load them into the last freight car."

The carriage began jogging again. When it stopped, the blurred figure of a man opened the carriage door. He was stocky with large, strong arms.

"You must each crawl inside one of these sacks," he said gently, tossing two gunny sacks into the carriage and then closing the door.

But he continued speaking. "You can breathe through

the sacks and stretch around a bit when we put you in the freight car. Hang limp when we carry you."

The girls stepped inside the sacks and began pulling them over their bodies and then over their heads. Outside they could hear the hissing steam of the train engine and the bang and shove of heavy freight cars.

"I don't like bein' tied up in a sack, Julilly." Liza scowled and there was a look of terror in her eyes. But she pulled the harsh cloth over her head and sat waiting in the carriage seat. Julilly did the same.

The driver opened the door and crawled inside. He tied each sack tightly at the top. Then he picked up Liza and handed her to his waiting helper outside.

"Make yourself as small as possible," he told Julilly, "and I will carry you over my shoulder."

Julilly knew if she stretched out she would be twice as long as Liza. She huddled together as best she could.

A swirling sound of people and train noises, together with the drip of steady rain, surrounded Julilly. She felt the arms of the driver tighten about her.

A voice cried out above the confusion:

"Search all those cars for runaway slaves."

Julilly's heart pounded. She was glad for the sack and glad for the protecting arms around her.

"Two packages of dry goods go in this car," she heard another voice call.

She was lifted into the car and carried far back into

what must have been a dark corner. She was placed next to the sack that was Liza.

"Don't move and don't talk until the train starts," the driver said softly. "You're going to Cleveland. A friend of the Underground Railway will meet you there. It's best you stay in the sacks until you reach your destination. But I'll loosen the top so you can stick your heads out for the trip."

He pulled the cloth down from the girls' heads, but it was so dark they could barely see each other. The car began to move and the man left quickly.

There was a screech and the banging of a door. Wheels creaked and rolled beneath them. The car jerked and the girls fell against each other. A bell clanged. The train was frightening with its strange urgency. The wheels turned fast and then faster, clicking over the long, silver track. Julilly pictured it in her mind. It would look like the track they had walked along in the state of Kentucky. The sound and speed of the wheels began humming inside Julilly's head. She felt dizzy. Liza groaned each time the big empty freight car rattled and jerked.

Julilly grew thirsty. Her mouth was dry and her tongue felt thick. She began to think about the rain outside and how she wanted it to pound through the car and wash down over her. She leaned against Liza.

"Julilly," Liza mumbled, "I think my own bones has come loose, and is rattlin' around in this sack."

Julilly had no answer. The train rattled on and on. It was going on for ever, she began to think, and with all this speed it might fly right off the tracks. Julilly forgot about a destination and that sometime the train would have to stop.

She dozed off to sleep for a time, and was surprised when their freight car banged into the car ahead of them and the rhythm of the wheels became slower and slower and then stopped.

"Liza!" Julilly cried out in alarm, feeling her friend's body slumped against her legs.

"I'm not dead," Liza groaned. "I just can't sit up."

In the middle of the car a light appeared. The door of their car slowly opened and a wild whip of cold fresh air blew in around them.

"I am seeking two parcels of dry goods shipped to me from Cincinnati," a familiar voice called out. "I will take care of their transfer aboard the schooner *Mayflower* personally."

Julilly remembered. The voice belonged to Massa Ross from Canada! He must have escaped from jail. He had come, as he promised, to take them into the land of freedom.

"Ah, here they are!" he cried. He leaned over the girls without speaking and quickly tied the sacks over their heads. Then he picked up a girl in each strong arm and strode from the car. Within minutes he lifted them into a carriage with heavy drawn curtains. He untied the sacks at once and pulled the girls free from them.

Liza fell onto the floor. She was too twisted and bent to sit on the seat. Julilly stooped to lift her and came face to face with Massa Ross. But was it Massa Ross? He had no beard; his hair was dark red but shorter; his chest and stomach were puffed out round and full as before, but the clothes that covered them were plain. The ruffled shirt was gone.

He rubbed his smooth chin and his eyes crinkled with laughter.

"Julilly and Liza." His voice was muffled but still lofty as though he might be preaching a sermon. "Praise God that you have overcome innumerable hardships and are now on the very brink of freedom."

"A drink, Massa Ross." Julilly could barely manage the words. Her mouth had the dryness of dust on the Mississippi road to the cotton fields.

"My dear children." The large man heaved himself down to a bag at his feet. He pulled out a bottle and unscrewed a cap. Water gurgled into a cup.

"Liza first," Julilly said.

Mr. Ross held Liza upright and lifted the cup to her lips.

"Drink slowly, child," he said. "When your body has been drained of moisture, it cannot stand the shock of unlimited amounts."

Soon the cup came to Julilly. The moisture cooled her lips. She held the liquid in her mouth. It trickled down her throat and she swallowed twice, greedily.

"There will be more when you board the *Mayflower*." Mr. Ross bent down and returned the bottle to the leather bag.

Now that her mind was released from the dreadful thirst, Julilly realized that the carriage was moving. She could see only the outlines of Mr. Ross' face in the seat opposite her and Liza. Liza clutched the seat with both hands, struggling painfully to straighten her back.

"Freedom ain't easy, Massa Ross." Liza sounded again like the sullen, angry girl of the long-ago slave cabin on the Riley plantation. "Even you got put in jail, and your face don't look so well."

Mr. Ross was weary. He leaned his head back against the carriage seat.

"They had to release me when the slave whose disappearance caused my trial returned. He came into the courtroom just when I was about to be condemned."

Mr. Ross spoke again, but quieter this time:

"Injustice is the weapon of evil men. But there are always brave and noble souls who proceed on the course of right and are impervious to the consequences. I feel rewarded for all my efforts, just to free the two of you."

Julilly was pleased with the ring of his words. Whatever Massa Ross was saying, it helped her lift her head and straighten her back and think of Mammy Sally, who never bent low to anyone.

Julilly thought back to the hot day in the cotton fields, when Massa Ross marched down the rows and chose Lester and then Adam to be his guides. Lester and Adam! Why hadn't she and Liza asked about them right away. Massa Ross would know where they were.

"Massa Ross," Julilly blurted out in a jumble of fear and hope, "did Lester and Adam get to Canada?"

Mr. Ross leaned forward slowly.

"They reached Canada, all right," he said. "They both knew freedom."

He paused. "Lester has a job in the town of St. Catharines. He wants both of you to come there . . . Adam died."

There was a shocked moment of silence.

Kind, gentle Adam. Julilly felt the dryness again in her throat, but this time there was throbbing pain. Liza bent forward, straining her crippled back. Her eyes filled with tears, which ran freely over her scarred black cheeks.

"How did he die, Massa Ross?" she asked.

Mr. Ross' shoulders slumped. "It was the chains." His voice was husky. "They were too tight and cut through the flesh. When we filed them off, there was blood poisoning. Adam lived in Canada only one day. We buried him under a tall pine tree."

There was nothing more to say. The evil chains. Julilly

felt herself wanting to pry them apart for ever—to strain every muscle in her body to pull every chain loose from the legs, and arms, and necks of every slave.

The carriage stopped and Julilly wiped the tears from her face with the sleeve of her newly-knitted sweater. Before she heard about Adam, Julilly was going to ask Massa Ross if he had seen a tall, black-skinned woman with a proud walk who went by the name of Mammy Sally. Now she was afraid to know.

The carriage jolted. The door opened and the girls with Mr. Ross stepped into a dusky, lead-grey street. It was evening. To be safe, they pulled their new hats far down over the blackness of their faces. They tucked their hands under the warmth of the wisteria-blue sweaters.

Before them was a vast, grey stretch of water. It didn't have the sound of the rolling Mississippi. The water heaved and pushed toward the shore and then splashed in one long row of waves. Great hulks of boats, anchored along its sides, rocked with the rhythm of the moving water. On one of the largest, the sails were being pulled aloft.

"That one is the *Mayflower*—the Abolition Boat," Mr. Ross said. "It will take you across Lake Erie to Canada under its waving sails."

"Then you aren't comin' with us?" Julilly faced him soberly.

Mr. Ross heaved his great shoulders and breathed long and full into the vastness of his chest. "I must return again to the South and free more of your people," he said. He picked up the skimpy bundles from the carriage floor and walked toward the boat.

"Keep your caps pulled down and don't raise your heads to look at anyone," Mr. Ross turned and whispered to the girls. "With those new clothes a passer-by would think you were my children. It's fortunate the day is grey and cloudy."

It was only a few steps to the boat and at once Mr. Ross began shaking the hand of a man he called "the Captain." Mr. Ross didn't raise his voice with his usual flourish but spoke quietly.

"A friend with friends," he said at first. The magic password of the Underground Railroad. Julilly felt warm and excited each time she heard it.

"These are my children," Mr. Ross continued. "Take them safely to Fort Malden."

The captain was a jolly man with a hat cocked to one side of his head.

"Aye, that I will." He hung onto each word with peals of laughter. "Come with me, lads, to your bunks below."

Mr. Ross patted each girl gently on the shoulder and bade them good-bye. He disappeared into the grey evening dusk. Julilly and Liza wanted to call out to thank this big, kind man. But both of them knew the need for silence. It would be dangerous, too, for them and for Mr. Ross if they lifted their heads and showed their black faces.

The girls walked aboard the *Mayflower* with the Captain. Julilly felt the boat must be breathing and that she was walking over its body. It went up and down with each rise and fall of the waves beneath it. They followed the Captain down a narrow flight of stairs and then walked along a corridor with tiny doors on either side. At one of them they stopped. The Captain opened the door to a little room. It was

hardly big enough for the three of them to stand inside. Two beds seemed to hang on the side of the wall and a small round window looked out on the water.

"I know ye are lassies," the Captain laughed again, "but for this trip ye will be laddies to me and me mates."

He showed the girls how to lock their door and warned them to open it only when they heard three knocks and then the words "a friend with friends." He would bring them food and water at once. Then they were to crawl into their beds and sleep with all their clothing on.

"If all goes well"—the Captain smiled broadly beneath his thick black moustache—"we will reach the banks of Canada in the early morning light." The r's in his speech trilled together like the song of a bird, Julilly thought. She would have no trouble recognizing his voice behind a door that was closed.

The Captain bent down and walked out of the little door. The girls locked it behind them.

18

There was barely time for Julilly and Liza to look about the cabin, when three raps were heard on the door, and the Captain's voice whispered,

"A friend with friends. Open the door, lassies, there's trouble aboard."

Julilly turned the lock. The Captain's face puffed with anger.

"I've had word there's a slave hunter and sheriff coming aboard, with a warrant to search the schooner before we set sail." He peered closely at the girls.

"I've a notion that ye're the lassies they're making all the stir about."

He picked up their bundles and hurried them out of the door. They ran down the narrow corridor and up the winding stairs. It was nearly dark on the open deck. Firefly-looking lanterns bobbed here and there. The wind was full of the smell of fish, and it was cold.

The girls ran with the Captain across the deck to the

far side of the schooner where a little life-boat, covered with canvas, hung against the side. The Captain pulled back the canvas and helped Julilly and Liza inside.

"Ye'll find blankets, water, and a bite of food in there. Take care and pray that the Good Lord will protect ye." He pulled down the canvas and left them alone.

The girls shivered. They felt about for the blankets and crawled under them, partly for warmth and partly for protection.

"We're gonna jump into the water," Julilly said solemnly, "if that sheriff comes near this little boat and takes the canvas off the top."

Liza clutched Julilly's shoulder.

"We're never goin' back to bein' slaves again."

It was a pledge between them. They were near the end of their journey. Massa Ross had said that Canada and freedom were on the other side of Lake Erie. There was no more walking through the woods, or climbing mountains, or hiding in wet swamp water.

"After all our trials, Liza," Julilly said slowly, "anythin' is better than goin' back to slavery."

There was a small opening between the canvas and the top of their little boat, and the girls found that by looking through it they could see onto the deck.

People walked aboard with baskets and bundles in their arms. Sailors pulled at ropes and lifted rolls of heavy white cloth. Near the plank where the people came on board, the Captain stood scowling—his cap still pulled down over one eye and his moustache looking stiff and forbidding.

The girls kept their eyes on him. Two large men shoved their way up the plank and approached him. They could be the sheriff and the slave hunter. Julilly and Liza didn't know. They had never seen them before. The men spoke to the Captain, waving their arms in his face and pacing impatiently up and down beside him. They seemed like horses pawing the ground, wanting some kind of action. But the words they spoke were lost to Liza and Julilly in the wind and the splashing noise of lapping water.

The Captain shook his head. He threw his arms into the air as though in despair. He walked toward the thin stairway. The big men followed.

"They are going to search the cabins, Liza!" Julilly gasped, realizing just how lucky their escape had been. "We're gonna get to Canada, if we've got to hang onto the bottom of this boat and get pulled across Lake Erie." Julilly was angry now. What right had these men to keep chasing them right up to the border, as if they were two runaway dogs? She and Liza were not going to be slaves no more.

It was night now. The grey fringes of daylight had slipped from the sky. Dark clouds foamed and raced above the *Mayflower*. Then they parted and a half-moon dazzled the schooner with yellow light. The North Star shone above with radiant steadiness. A bell clanged and the boat swayed impatiently as though eager to break away from the shore.

The Captain and the two large men popped out of the stairway. They heaved and puffed and ran to the entrance plank. They shook their fists in the Captain's face, but he shoved them onto the plank and waved good-bye.

The *Mayflower* turned. It swung around into the wind. The sails high above began cutting through the water.

"I feel that I'm flyin' through the sky just like those sails." Liza hugged Julilly as they both pushed a wider opening in the canvas so they could see more of the outside.

The joy that Julilly felt was so intense that there was pain around her heart.

"Liza," Julilly said finally, "Mammy Sally is watchin' that same North Star. I've got to keep myself from hopin' too much, but I'm hopin' that it's led her to freedom, too."

Liza began feeling about for the bundle of food and the flask of water. The girls ate and drank all of it. They drew the blankets close around them and watched the billowing sails catch the rushing wind.

Without wanting to, they slept in the hollow shelter of the small life-boat. When the Captain found them later, peaceful and warm, he left them to rock through the night and be refreshed for the morning.

A CRISP, BRIGHT MORNING came quickly with thin, white frost powdering the deck. The air was strong with fresh fish smells. They mixed with the land smells of pine and pungent walnut bark and fertile earth still warm from summer. The waves on Lake Erie lapsed into gentle ripples. Sails were pulled in and the *Mayflower* drifted ashore.

Julilly and Liza woke with the sudden stillness of the schooner's landing. They grasped each other's hand for comfort, at once remembering the *Mayflower*, Lake Erie, and their nearness to Canada.

They pushed up the canvas on their little boat and the bright sun showered over them. The Captain ran toward them shouting with his trilling r's and upturned sentences.

"Ahoy." He waved for the girls to join him. "All passengers ashore."

He grabbed the girls by their arms and ushered them down the plank to the shoreline. He pointed to rows of tall, silent trees and the long, bleak shore.

"See those trees," he shouted. "They grow on free soil."

Julilly and Liza ran down the plank and jumped to the ground.

"Canada?" they cried together.

The Captain nodded.

Liza dropped to her knees. She spread out her arms and kissed the ground. "Bless the Lord, I'm free!" she cried.

Julilly stood as tall and straight as she could. She pulled the cap from her head and held her head high. There was no longer any need to hide her black skin. She was Julilly, a free person. She was not a slave.

"Thank you, Lord," she said aloud. She filled her lungs as full as she could with the air of this new free land. No one else was near them except the Captain, who was wiping tears from his eyes and blowing his nose. But he seemed nervous and jumpy and kept watching each passenger who walked from the schooner.

"Ye are safe now," he said warmly to the girls, "and it does me heart good to have brought ye here." Then he lowered his voice. "But ye must remember that I must go back to Ohio this very day. I can't be getting myself arrested for helping slaves escape to freedom, and I can't be revealing that I'm a 'conductor' on the Underground Railway, even though my part of the train goes on top of the water." He laughed suddenly.

Julilly looked at the Captain with new admiration. In her great joy to be standing on the soil of Canada, she had forgotten how this man was risking his job and maybe his life to bring them across Lake Erie on the *Mayflower*.

"Liza and I will never forget how you and all the people of the Underground Railway helped us, Captain," Julilly said. She wanted to give him something, but her bundle was limp and empty.

Liza seemed not to hear them. She was still kneeling on the ground praying.

"I'm giving ye a little money from Mr. Ross," said the Captain, awkwardly shoving some paper bills into Julilly's hand. "Far down the shore there is a coloured man with a cart waiting to take ye and your friend to the town of St. Catharines. Mr. Ross arranged it. Your cousin Lester has a job in that town and he'll take care of ye for a bit."

Julilly looked quickly down the long stretch of rocks and sand that ran beside the lapping blue water of the great Lake Erie, and, sure enough, there was a man with a cart waiting beside one of the roads.

19

The captain turned swiftly and ran back to his schooner.

Small clusters of people gathered here and there along the quiet shore. But Julilly felt no need to be greeted by anyone. She began to hum softly as the words rang in her head,

Swing low, sweet chariot.
Coming for to carry me home . . .

Julilly walked toward Liza and shook her gently on the shoulder.

"You can't just sit here prayin' for the rest of your life, Liza," Julilly laughed with a full, strong voice. "We've a ways to go yet and there's a man right up there waitin' to take us there."

Liza seemed dazed. But she stood without help from Julilly and the two of them walked silently round the shoreline toward the coloured man, whose wagon was hitched to an aged brown horse.

As they neared him, he seemed to recognize them as his passengers, and stood waving them toward him.

Liza drew back. "We'd best hide in those bushes, Julilly, until it's dark. What's he mean, lettin' everyone see him wavin' at us."

"Liza." Julilly shook her friend again. "We are in Canada, and we are free, and free means not havin' to hide no more."

Liza stopped in shocked amazement as though this new idea struck her like a bolt of lightning.

"You is right, Julilly," Liza said and her back seemed to straighten a little with almost no expression of pain on her face. "We can walk right up to that cart and climb on board and lift up our heads, just like the white people always do."

The kindly brown-skinned driver climbed down and held out both his hands. He was tall and strong and his hair bushed out from his head like a grey and black speckled frame.

"I'm Ezra Wilson," he said, smiling as though the sun had lighted his face with a spark. "Massa Ross sent word you were comin' and Lester said I was to bring you right to him in St. Catharines." He reached for Julilly's hand and then Liza's and held them tight.

The girls were speechless, until Liza's sullen eyes suddenly sparkled.

"I was sort of expectin' that Queen Victoria herself might be marchin' up and down this shore when we arrived," she said, "but I think, Ezra Wilson, that you look just as good."

Ezra Wilson chuckled, but continued to hold their hands.

"I know how you feel," he nodded quietly. "I came here last year, just like you, at the time of the harvest."

"We'd best not talk now." The tall, strong man turned from them and began to busy himself with the fresh straw and blankets in the back of the cart. "It's a two-day trip to St. Catharines. We'll have plenty of time to say a good many things by then."

The girls climbed into the cart and settled themselves on the straw. It was too warm for the blankets now. The morning sun had a soothing warmth. There was a burnished glow about it, like the ripened skin of a red apple.

Ezra Wilson sat above them and flicked the reins for the horse to go. The cart began to jog up a steep road, lined on either side by tall, green pines.

The two days of travel along the country roads of Upper Canada with kindly Ezra Wilson were a time of peace and quiet joy for Julilly and Liza.

At first they covered themselves with the blankets when other people came their way. But no one stopped them, and no one shouted, and when they came to the small towns and were hungry, they walked into the stores and bought food with the money Massa Ross had given them. At night, when the sun disappeared, they felt the hard cold of this new north country. Then the blankets warmed them and they were never afraid.

On the second morning the leaves on the trees beside their jogging cart were yellow-gold. Ezra Wilson stopped and spread a blanket beneath them and they ate their lunch.

"It's like heaven here," Liza murmured softly.

Ezra Wilson stood up abruptly.

"No, it isn't heaven," he said curtly, "and I've got to tell you how it is." He looked at the girls a long time and then continued. "We coloured folks in St. Catharines work hard, very hard. But we've got food to eat and most of us have a warm, dry place to live."

Julilly looked at him with apprehension. What else did he have to tell them to let them know that Canada wasn't just a place with yellow-gold leaves?

Ezra continued to stand. His face was stern but he didn't raise his voice.

"We've found jobs," he said, "but none of us can read, and all the white folks can."

"Read?" Julilly asked, never having thought in all her life that she might ever learn to read.

"It seems, Liza and Julilly, that the white folks don't want us in their schools." Ezra's face grew sad. There's a

St. Paul's Ward School in St. Catharines for the coloured and a St. Paul's Ward School for the whites; and the white school's got more books and more paper and more desks, and a good strong building."

"But can we go to school and learn to read?" Julilly's eyes grew round with wonder.

"Would they let somebody like me come?" Liza lifted herself painfully to look up into the face of tall Ezra Wilson.

"I'm learnin." Ezra smiled down at her and rubbed his grey-flecked hair. "Now I guess I'll just end all this warnin' talk by sayin' that I made up my mind that salt and potatoes in Canada are better than pound-cake and chickens in a state of worry and suspense in the United States. Now, let's eat lunch."

While he talked, Julilly remembered what Massa Ross had told them a long time ago in Mississippi—that escaping into Canada would be hard and that living in Canada would be hard, too. But it didn't seem to hurt to remember this. She and Liza could work, and salt and potatoes weren't bad for eating when no slave owner was around to threaten or whip.

One night Ezra Wilson talked about St. Catharines . . . how Lester worked there as a porter in the Welland House Hotel where a special pipe brought magic mineral water to all the guests. He told how former slaves helped to build the hotel, and how many of them worked there now.

"It's a grand place." Ezra spread his long arms wide and high. "A big porch runs along the front of it, and all the fine people sit there rockin' away in their chairs."

Julilly and Liza were excited and yet worried about arriving in the town. They talked continually to one another in the jogging wagon. How would it be to live in a town and not be a slave? How would Lester look? If only Adam had lived to welcome them, too.

Julilly yearned to ask Ezra Wilson if he had ever seen or heard of a handsome black woman called Mammy Sally. But she didn't dare. As long as no one had heard of her, there was always hope that she would come to Canada. But if they did know, and something bad had happened to her, Julilly wanted to put off the knowing of it as long as she could.

On the morning of the third day, Ezra told them that the town they were coming to was St. Catharines. At first it looked like the other villages they had travelled through. There were large and small houses, mostly built of brick. Trees and shrubs and flowers grew everywhere. But on the streets of St. Catharines were many black folks just like them. When they came to the part of the town where the shops were they saw many more.

"They aren't dressed fancy," Liza said to Julilly, "but they aren't wearin' rags."

At the end of the street they saw a large two-storey building with a wide porch running across the front of it—the Welland House Hotel. Ezra pulled in the reins to slow the horse. In front of the hotel stood a light-skinned coloured man with freckles. He wore a tight suit that buttoned up the front with shining gold buttons.

"It's Lester," Julilly shouted. She jumped from the wagon and ran toward him.

Lester grabbed both her hands in his and looked at her fondly. Julilly searched his face. Lester was well and content, but the anger was still in his eyes and the pride was still in his high-held head. Julilly was glad. The beatings and chains hadn't crushed him down like a snake.

Together they saw Liza trying to crawl over the back of the wagon. Lester ran toward her and picked her up in his arms. The three of them stood together for a moment in a tight happy circle. Tall, kind Ezra Wilson joined them. Then Lester placed Liza gently on the dirt road beneath them. As he did so, he glanced toward a door at the far end of the Hotel.

"You'll want to see her right away in the kitchen, Julilly," Lester said.

"Her? Kitchen?" Julilly was puzzled. Was it someone wanting to give her a job in the kitchen?

"It's a surprise I planned for you, Julilly," Lester said. "I made Ezra promise not to tell." Angry, hostile Lester became surprisingly sheepish.

A woman opened the far back door. Julilly stared. She

was tall and dark skinned with a white kerchief about her head. But her hair was grey. Her face was wrinkled. She was old. Then the woman came toward them—limping, but with long, full strides.

"Mammy Sally," Julilly cried and ran into her mother's outstretched arms.

"Child, child." Mammy Sally sang the words over and over again.

Finally she held Julilly at arm's length. Her eyes were radiant.

"June Lilly, you have grown." She looked again with grave concern. "You have become a woman."

Julilly didn't hear. Being with Mammy Sally again was like shifting a hundred-pound sack of cotton from her back and just taking on a two-pound load instead. But it also filled her heart with such a joy she wanted to shout and sing. Instead, Julilly put a strong arm around her mother to support her.

"How did you know, Mammy, how did you know to come out that door and meet me?" she asked.

"Land, child, didn't Massa Ross tell you I was here, or did Lester keep it a secret from him too?" Mammy Sally laughed and tears streamed down her cheeks.

Julilly remembered Liza. She led her mother to the hunched, thin girl who stood quietly on the road.

"Liza came with me," Julilly said simply to Mammy Sally. "We are like sisters."

Mammy Sally touched Liza gently on the head. "You gonna live with us, Liza. I'm buyin' us a little house." She stood proud and tall before all of them. "We'll walk there now."

They all started walking down the wide dirt road—Liza, Julilly, and Mammy Sally in the lead with Lester and Ezra behind them.

"We are free and we are together." Mammy Sally almost sang the words. Then she paused and looked long and joyfully at the strangely dressed girls beside her.

She started walking again and said,

"Freedom isn't easy. We black folks can't read and we can't write and the white people in St. Catharines don't want us in their schools . . . We are poor, but we are buildin' us a church and buildin' us a school. We are poor, but we get paid for the jobs we do. We are poor, but some of us are buildin' houses on the land we own. We are poor, but none of us is slaves."

Mammy Sally's words became a song. There was a rhythm and a rising cadence to each new line. They all began marching toward a grove of tall, green pines.

Julilly glanced at her mother's face. It had deep wrinkles. The hair that shone beneath her kerchief was powdery white with specks of grey. There were scars on Mammy's neck. She'd been lashed with a whip. She limped when she walked. But her head was high and her voice rang with courage and deep joy.

Julilly put a strong arm around her mother to support her. She pulled Liza along with her other hand.

Mammy Sally needed her. Liza and Lester needed her. She was growing up. There was a lot for her to do in this great new land of freedom.

ACKNOWLEDGMENTS

The quotation from Martin Luther King Jr. is taken from p. 1 of *Conscience for Change*, published by CBC Learning Systems in 1967—the printed form of the 1967 Massey Lectures. Reprinted by permission of the Canadian Broadcasting Corporation.

The spirituals on pages 8 and 22 appear respectively on p. 107 of *To Be a Slave* by Julius Lester (Dial Press, 1968) and on p. 315 of *Jubilee* by Margaret Walker (Houghton Mifflin, 1966).

The idea for the incident on pp. 103 to 109 was found in a description of the slave Magog on p. 134 of *Make Free—The Story of the Underground Railroad* by William Breyfogle (Lippincott, 1958).

I am indebted for the information on St. Catharines' history to *The Negroes of the Niagara Peninsula*, written by Ivan Grok, a retired history teacher in St. Catharines, Ontario.

Ezra Wilson's statement about "salt and potatoes

in Canada" on p. 164 is a direct quotation from *The Narratives of Fugitive Slaves in Canada* by Benjamin Drew, p. 39. (Facsimile edition published by Coles Publishing Co., Toronto, 1972.)

PUFFIN CLASSICS

Underground to Canada

With Puffin Classics, the adventure isn't
over when you reach the final page.
Want to discover more about your favourite
characters, their creators, and their worlds?
Read on

CONTENTS

AUTHOR FILE

WHO'S WHO IN *UNDERGROUND TO CANADA*

SOME THINGS TO THINK ABOUT ...

SOME THINGS TO DO ...

GLOSSARY

BIBLIOGRAPHY

NAME: Barbara Smucker
BORN: Newton, Kansas, in 1915
NATIONALITY: American and Canadian
LIVED: Many different places in the U.S.A. (Kansas, Mississippi, New Jersey, Illinois, Ohio) and in Ontario, Canada
DIED: Bluffton, Ohio, in 2003
MARRIED: Yes, to Donovan Smucker in 1939
CHILDREN: Timothy, Thomas, and Rebecca

What was she like?

Barbara cared deeply about social-justice issues: whether people had enough to eat, whether they were being forced to work unjustly or unsafely, and whether they had basic human rights. She was a Mennonite, a member of a religious group for whom social-justice issues are very important. Through her books, Barbara explored new ideas and tried to make people consider leaving behind old ways of thinking that were harmful.

Where did she grow up?

Barbara grew up in Newton, Kansas. She was the oldest child in her family and had three younger brothers. After finishing high school in Newton, she went to Kansas State University, where she got a degree in journalism.

What did she do apart from writing books?

Her husband's work moved the Smucker family around the U.S. and Canada a lot, but wherever Barbara was, she loved sharing ideas with people. When she wasn't writing books, she was working as a reporter, a children's librarian, and a teacher. At one point, she was the only white teacher in an all-black high school.

Where did she get the idea for Underground to Canada?

Underground to Canada linked Barbara's interest in social-justice issues with her love of exploring history—and her need to write strong, believable characters like Julilly and Liza.

What did people think of Underground to Canada?

People loved *Underground to Canada* from the moment it was published. Although it deals with a difficult time in North American history, when a lot of horrible things happened, there were also acts of incredible bravery and self-sacrifice that Barbara wanted to recognize. The book won lots of awards, was a bestseller in Canada, and was named one of the top fifty books of all time for young readers in Canada.

What other books did she write?

Barbara Smucker's books have been published in sixteen countries worldwide, and have been translated into French, German, Japanese, Swedish, Spanish, Dutch, and Danish. It's safe to say that lots of people really like her work! Here's a complete list:

Days of Terror
Selina and the Bear Paw Quilt

Selina and the Shoo-Fly Pie
Garth and the Mermaid
Amish Adventure
Henry's Red Sea
Jacob's Little Giant
Incredible Jumbo
White Mist

June Lilly / Julilly – a brave, strong-willed girl who's not afraid to take a chance to escape slavery in order to make a better life for herself. Born on Massa Hensen's plantation in Virginia, she is Liza's best friend and Mammy Sally's daughter. At the time the novel begins, she is twelve years old.

Liza – Julilly's best friend and companion on the dangerous journey North. Brutally beaten when she attempted to escape from Massa Riley's Mississippi plantation, she suffers from constant pain but is still determined to reach freedom in Canada. She is thirteen years old.

"Aunt Katie" / Catherine Coffin – Levi Coffin's wife. She is an Abolitionist and helps shelter slaves on the Underground Railroad.

Adam – a gentle young man with a beautiful voice who is sold away from his wife and family to go South to the Riley plantation.

Alexander Milton Ross – an Abolitionist who poses as an ornithologist in order to pass the word about the Underground Railroad to slaves throughout the southern United States.

Ben – a tall, strong young man from the Hensen plantation who is sold South with Julilly to the Riley plantation. He too is taken away from his wife and children.

Bessie – a young girl on the Riley plantation.

Ella Brown – owner of a way station on the Underground Railroad in Covington, Tennessee, and Jeb's wife.

Ezra Wilson – an older man who has travelled the Underground Railroad to freedom and now lives in St. Catharines, Ontario.

Grannie – the old woman in charge of babies and toddlers at the Riley plantation.

James – a young boy who works for Mr. Fox.

Jeb Brown – owner of a way station on the Underground Railroad in Covington, Tennessee, and Ella's husband.

Joe – an old man who helps Julilly and Liza on their trek out of the Appalachian Mountains.

Lester – a courageous, angry young man who is torn from his wife and family when he is sold to Massa Riley. He and Julilly form a close bond, and his anger gives her the strength to keep going.

Levi Coffin – the "president" of the Underground Railroad, who operates a way station in Cincinnati, Ohio.

Lily Brown – a teenage mother on the Hensen plantation whose toddler son, Willie, is sold away from her.

Mammy Sally – Julilly's mother, who works in the Hensens' kitchen. Strong, dignified, and fearless, she is the only parent Julilly has ever known. Remembering her songs helps Julilly during the dangerous journey to Canada.

Massa (Master) Jeb Hensen – the owner of the Hensen plantation, where Julilly was born.

Massa (Master) Riley – the owner of the Riley plantation.

Missy Hensen – Massa Jeb Hensen's wife.

Mr. Fox – an Abolitionist whom Julilly and the Hensen plantation slaves meet along the way to the Riley plantation.

Old John – The Hensens' coachman.

Sheriff Donnelly – the sheriff of Cincinnati, Ohio, and a runaway slave hunter.

Sheriff Starkey – the sheriff of Covington, Tennessee, and a runaway slave hunter.

Sims – the brutal overseer of the Riley plantation, who takes Julilly and the other Hensen-plantation workers away from their home.

The Captain – the skipper of the *Mayflower*, a sailing ship that crosses Lake Erie.

The Mennonites – the people of Felsheim, Tennessee, who help Julilly and Liza by feeding and sheltering them.

The Quaker – an unnamed Abolitionist who hides the runaways and gives them a compass.

Willie Brown – a toddler who is sold away from Lily, his teenage mother, when the Hensen plantation is dissolved.

Alexander Milton Ross – a naturalist and physician, was born on December 13, 1832, at Belleville, Upper Canada, and died in Detroit, Michigan, on October 27, 1897.

> In undertaking this mission to help the slaves to freedom I did not disguise from myself the dangers I would most certainly have to encounter, and the certainty that a speedy and perhaps cruel death would be my lot in case my plans and purposes were discovered.*
>
> Alexander M. Ross

An outspoken abolitionist . . . was Alexander Milton Ross. . . . In 1855, when he was 23, he decided upon an active career of running fugitives from the deep South to Canada. Ross made at least five trips to the southern states, posing as a bird-watcher; and in five years he was instrumental to the escape of 31 or more blacks . . . John Greenleaf Whittier dedicated one of his poems to Ross.†

* *Memoirs of a Reformer* by Alexander M. Ross. p. 41
† *The Blacks in Canada* by Robin W. Winks, p. 260

There died in the city of Detroit, on October 27, 1897, a man whose services in the abolition movement and during the Civil War were of so self-sacrificing and daring a character they gained for him the tributes not only of the abolition leaders but of Lincoln himself. Alexander Milton Ross, M.D., Canadian by birth . . . had a career that deserves to be better known . . . Wendell Phillips declared, "No higher heroism, courage or tenacity of purpose was ever displayed than by you in your chivalric efforts to help the slaves to freedom."*

He was a distinguished ornithologist, cited by European governments and learned societies for original and painstaking work on birds of North America. . . . His Canadian accent made him supposedly a neutral in internal affairs of the U.S. and letters of introduction established him as a naturalist of international standing . . . Wandering through fields and woods in the South, he had a rare opportunity to talk to slaves, to provide them with a little money, and information on how to travel and where to stop.†

Levi Coffin – a businessman, Quaker leader and Abolitionist, was born in 1798 in New Garden, N. Carolina, and died in Cincinnati, Ohio, in 1877.

> I am opposed to the whole system of slavery, and conscientiously believe it to be a sin against God and a crime against

* "A Daring Canadian Abolitionist" by Fred Landon, librarian at London, Ontario, article in the *Michigan History Magazine*, 1921, p. 364

† *Make Free—The Story of the Underground Railroad* by William Breyfogle, p. 190

man to channelize a human being and reduce God's image to the level of a brute, to be bought and sold in the market as cattle or swine.*

Levi Coffin

Levi Coffin, by his devotion to the cause of the fugitive from boyhood to old age, gained the title of President of the Underground Railroad, but he was not at the head of a formal organization. In truth the work was everywhere spontaneous. Unfaltering confidence among members of neighbouring stations served better than a code of rules . . . decision and sagacity of the individual was required rather than the less rapid efforts of an organization.†

He and his wife aided more than 3,000 slaves in flight.‡

For 33 years, he and his wife, Catherine, received into their home in Newport, Ind., and Cincinnati, O., more than 100 slaves every year.§

---

* From a letter quoted in *The Underground Railroad—From Slavery to Freedom* by Wilbur Siebert, p. 592

† Ibid., p. 69

‡ Ibid., p. 87

§ Ibid., p. 111

Sims and the slave hunters don't see Julilly, Liza, and their friends as human beings. Why do you think they feel this way? Do you think they could ever have "walked a mile" in Julilly's shoes? Why or why not? What do you think would have to change before they could see Julilly as another human being, not just property to be bought and sold?

Has anything ever happened to you or to your friends just because of your skin colour or cultural background? How did you or your friends deal with that situation? And how did it make you feel?

The word "nigger" is used a lot in the book, because that's what people said at the time, but it's now a hateful word you shouldn't use. However, some musicians still use it in their lyrics. Why do you think some people still use it? Do you think it is different if a black person uses it instead of a white person? If so, why? Or do you think that it's just a really bad word that shouldn't be used by anyone?

At several times during the novel, Julilly and Liza are pushed to their limit and just want to give up, but they keep going, despite how terrible they feel. Have you ever been pushed to your limit? Did you give up or keep going? And what made you give up or keep going?

Some of the gossip that Julilly and Liza hear about Canada is frightening: that nothing can grow there but black-eyed peas, that Canada is so cold in winter that the birds have to leave. But they decide to go anyway. Have you ever faced something unknown and frightening? How did you prepare for it? And how did you feel once it happened? Liza tells the story about how her father was whipped for buying a spelling book and trying to teach himself how to read. Why do you think this happened? And what do you think it says about the power of language?

Now we have laws that prevent most of the serious injustices portrayed in this story: long hours of work with not enough breaks, physical abuse, and child labour. Do you think we've done enough to protect workers? If not, what more can we do? What should we in wealthy countries do about bad practices in countries that don't have laws in place to protect workers?

Lester is frequently described as being angry, and during the journey from the Riley plantation, Julilly draws strength from his anger. Do you think that anger is the best reaction to injustice? Are Julilly and Liza angry? What about Alexander Ross?

Julilly and Liza do a lot of thinking and dreaming about what it will be like to be free, but when they finally get to Canada, both Ezra Wilson and Mammy Sally tell them that freedom isn't easy. What do you think that means? Does freedom mean something different for everyone, or are there degrees of freedom?

One of the passwords used by escaping slaves and the people who help them on the Underground Railroad is "friends with a friend." How does the idea of friendship show itself throughout the story? Do you think people have to know each other for a long time to be true friends, or can strangers be friends?

Try using a star chart or a "SkyView" app at night to see if you can find the Big Dipper. Where is it in the sky? How hard is it to see? How do you think you would follow it while walking—or if the weather got bad and you couldn't see it?

Songs and music were very important to the slave community. They were used to pass along coded messages as well as to keep up the people's hopes and spirits. Find other examples of spirituals and slave songs that contain messages—search "spirituals" on YouTube for some good ones—and then write your own coded song or poem.

Julilly's home plantation was in Virginia, but she made it all the way to St. Catharines, Ontario. Using GoogleEarth or an atlas, trace the path she and Liza took to freedom—or make a route of your own. Draw the route and try to think about how long it would have taken—but don't forget, Julilly and Liza wouldn't have been using major roads. What kinds of animals and people would they have encountered? How would they have found food? You may add these things to the map if you want.

Imagine you're a conductor on the Underground Railroad. How would you organize your house to hide people, like the Browns and Coffins did? How would you feed and clothe them before sending them on to the next stop? Draw a plan of how and where you would shelter escaping slaves.

Adam suffered from blood poisoning after the chains rubbed his ankles raw—a condition that's dangerous but not always fatal today, thanks to antibiotics. What other illnesses did people get in the 1800s that we don't often see today? What were the treatments? Do some research online or at the library to find out.

Sometimes Liza and Julilly had to escape in a huge hurry with nothing more than the clothes on their backs. If a disaster happened to you and you suddenly had to leave your home, what would you take with you? Which one of your personal things means the most to you? What couldn't you leave behind? Make a list of things you'd take with you and why (all of them should be able to fit in a backpack you can easily carry).

Since it stretched through so many U.S. states and up to Canada, the Underground Railroad was a very important part of American and Canadian history. Check out online resources like these to get a better picture of just how big the Underground Railroad really was:

http://www.nationalgeographic.com/railroad
A website from *National Geographic* with an interactive game involving an escape to Canada via the Underground Railroad.

http://quest.arc.nasa.gov/ltc/special/mlk/gourd2.html
A web page explaining the meaning behind the song "Follow the Drinking Gourd" as it led slaves to freedom. "Follow the Drinking Gourd" is mentioned in the epigraph by Martin Luther King Jr. that appears at the beginning of *Underground to Canada*.

http://blackhistorycanada.ca
A good site exploring all aspects of the history of black people in Canada.

http://www.pc.gc.ca/canada/proj/cfc-ugrr/index_e.asp
A major site by Parks Canada, emphasizing the Underground Railroad's presence and impact in Canada, with details on related National Historic Sites.

http://www.freedomtrail.ca/home.html
A highly illustrated site with loads of information on the places where ex-slaves settled in Ontario, including St. Catharines.

http://www.waynet.org/levicoffin
A site with interesting photos of Levi Coffin's house in Fountain City, Indiana. Although this is not the house portrayed in *Underground to Canada*, which was in Cincinnati (where the Coffins moved in 1847), this site gives a good idea of how the Coffins hid escaping slaves.

http://www.nps.gov/history/nr/travel/underground/ugrrhome.htm
A terrific site from the United States National Parks Service with details of historic sites in the U.S.A. that are associated with the Underground Railroad.

http://www.biographi.ca/EN/ShowBio.asp?BioId=40530
A Library and Archives Canada biography of Alexander Ross.

Abolitionist – a person who supported the destruction (or "abolition") of slavery in the nineteenth and twentieth centuries

boll – the round seed pod of the cotton plant

cat-o'-nine-tails – a whip made of nine separate ropes tied together; each rope has a thick knot tied at the end

cicada – an insect that makes a high-pitched sound with its large wings

collard greens – a big-leafed, slightly bitter plant in the cabbage family

cotton gin – a machine that separates cotton seeds from the cotton fibres

crocker sack – a cheap bag made of fibre, usually used to carry potatoes or grains; also called a gunny sack

cypress – a type of evergreen tree with scaly, overlapping needles

feather tick – an old-fashioned mattress made of feathers

field hand – a slave whose job is to work in the plantation fields

ginhouse – the building where the cotton gin operates

gourd – the dry, hollowed-out fruit of a plant in the squash family; often used as a drinking vessel

gunny sack – a cheap bag made of fibre, usually used to carry potatoes or grains; also called a crocker sack

hoecake – a flat bread made of cornmeal that was usually fried; also called johnny cake

honeysuckle – a vine or shrub with trumpet-shaped flowers that can be pink, red, white, or yellow

magnolia – a tree or shrub with beautiful pinkish-white fragrant flowers

mockingbird – a grey songbird with the ability to mimic many other bird songs and human noises

North Star – a bright star at the end of the "handle" of the Little Dipper constellation; also called Polaris

ornithologist – a scientist who studies birds

plantation – a large estate or farm on which crops like tobacco, cotton, or sugar cane are raised

Quaker – a member of the Religious Society of Friends, a religious group that believes in all kinds of social reform

rattan – a climbing palm plant with a tough, slim stem

schooner – a sailing ship with two or more masts

sowbelly – salt pork taken from the belly of a pig

straw tick – an old-fashioned mattress made of straw

Underground Railroad – a top-secret, loosely organized system for helping slaves escape to Canada or safe areas in the northern states

water-moccasin – a brown, tree-climbing swamp snake that is very poisonous; also called cottonmouth

whippoorwill – a spotted brown night bird that has a distinctive song

BIBLIOGRAPHY

Beattie, Jessie L., *Black Moses, the Real Uncle Tom*, The Ryerson Press, Toronto, 1957

Bolka, B. A. (ed.), *Lay My Burden Down—A Folk History of Slavery*, University of Chicago Press, 1969

Breyfogle, William, *Make Free—The Story of the Underground Railroad*, Lippincott, 1958

Browin, Frances Williams, *Looking for Orlando*, Criterion Books, 1961

Buckmaster, Henrietta, *Flight to Freedom*, Crowell, 1958

Coffin, Levi, *Reminiscences*, Arno Press and *The New York Times*, 1968 (reprinted from a copy in the Moorland-Springarn Collection, written in 1876)

Drew, Benjamin, *The Narratives of Fugitive Slaves in Canada*, John P. Jewett and Co., Cleveland, 1856. Facsimile edition by Coles Publishing Co., Toronto, 1972

Fradin, Dennis Brindell, *Bound for the North Star: True Stories of Fugitive Slaves*, Clarion Books, 2000

Gara, Larry, *The Liberty Line—The Legend of the Underground Railroad*, University of Kentucky Press, Lexington, 1967

Garrighan, Sally, *The Glass Door*, Doubleday, 1962

Greenwood, Barbara, *The Last Safe House: A Story of the Underground Railroad*, Kids Can Press, 1998

Lester, Julius, *To Be a Slave*, Dial Press, 1968

Levine, Ellen, *Henry's Freedom Box: A True Story from the Underground Railroad*, Scholastic, 2008

Prince, Bryan, *I Came as a Stranger: The Underground Railroad*, Tundra Books, 2004

Ross, Alexander Milton, *Recollections and Experiences of an Abolitionist*, Rowsell and Hutchison, Toronto 1875

Ross, Alexander Milton, *Memoirs of a Reformer*, Hunter, Rose & Co., Toronto, 1893

"The Search for a Black Past," *Life* magazine, November 22, 1968

Shadd, Adrienne, Afua Cooper, and Karolyn Smardz Frost, *The Underground Railroad: Next Stop, Toronto!*, Natural Heritage, 2005

Siebert, Wilbur H., *The Underground Railroad—From Slavery to Freedom*, Macmillan Co., 1898

Smedley, R. C., *History of the Underground Railroad*, Arno Press and *The New York Times*, 1969

Walker, Margaret, *Jubilee*, Houghton Mifflin, 1966

Winks, Robin W., *The Blacks in Canada, A History*, Yale University Press, 1971

Winks, Robin W. (gen. ed.), *Four Fugitive Slave Narratives*, Addison-Wesley Publishing Co., Reading, Mass., 1969